Other titles by the author

Ticket to Ride

We're gonna be famous

HATRED IS THE KEY

৪৩৫৪

Graham Sclater

Tabitha Books

ഇയ

On June 18, 1812, the United States declared war on Great Britain. Almost immediately they called for an invasion of Canada. The initial American successes turned to a number of defeats resulting in English ships effectively blockading the American coastline and subjecting it to a series of hit and run raids and the capture of numerous ships.

The majority of the crew captured from the American ships were transported to Plymouth in south west England to spend their time in the notorious Dartmoor depot, a prison constructed primarily to house 3,000 French prisoners-of-war. But by December 1814 there were more than 10,000 American prisoners incarcerated in what was the most evil of places.

80)08

Cover photography by Maureen Harrison

Author Graham Sclater is based in Devon where he works as a music publisher, songwriter and record producer. Prior to returning to Devon he was a professional musician playing and recording all over the world and working as a session musician with numerous artists. His first novel "Ticket to Ride" was published in 2006 followed by "We're gonna be famous" in 2009. He is currently working on a number of television series, screenplays and further novels.

80CR

Acknowledgements

Trevor and June James, Brett Johnson, Mike Chamberlain, David Keeling, Caroline Yeandle, Denise Bailey, Maureen Harrison and Feddy Lavrov, Brian Dingle at Dartmoor Prison Museum, Mr G L Johnson - Governor of HM Prison Dartmoor 2000 – 2002 and Andrea Bocelli for his wonderful music while I worked on this novel.

80CR

Dedicated to American prisoner-of-war John Seapatch,
aged 12, who died 7 February 1815 less than two months
after arriving in the Dartmoor depot

❧ Preface ❧

The early 1800's were a difficult time for England, already at war with France. The financial strain was further increased when it entered into a war with America.

The war of 1812, sometimes referred to as "the Second War of Independence" was fought between the United States and Great Britain from 1812 to 1814.

English ships instituted extensive maritime barricades of European ports to prevent American ships helping the French. The resulting seizure of American merchant shipping quickly brought demands for retaliation from the United States.

On June 18, 1812, the United States declared war on Great Britain. Almost immediately they called for an invasion of Canada. The initial American successes turned to a number of defeats resulting in English ships effectively blockading the American coastline and subjecting it to a series of hit and run raids and the capture of numerous ships.

In 1814 with France collapsing, Great Britain launched a number of major attacks on American cities, resulting in the burning of the White House and other public buildings. With America facing bankruptcy morale was extremely low.

The majority of the crew captured from the American ships were transported to Plymouth in south west England to spend their time in the notorious Dartmoor depot, a prison constructed primarily to house three thousand French prisoners-of-war, which was soon filled with 10,000 Americans.

80C3

HATRED IS THE KEY

Graham Sclater

৯০৫৪

✂ Chapter one ✂

The night sky was pitch black except for the curtain of shimmering stars.

The *Raytheon,* an impressive British ship of seventy four guns, sliced its way through the waves as it patrolled the east coast of the United States in search of any ship who dared to break the blockade.

The only movement on deck was the lone watchman, his footsteps, the creaking timbers and gently flapping sails gave a strange reassurance to all on board. He would stop periodically to shout to the lookout in the crows nest and peer out into the night looking for any sign of the enemy before continuing his ritualistic meandering.

The first pink fingers of dawn simmered on the horizon revealing the silhouette of a frigate and a much smaller brig. The night watchman reached the bow of the ship and, after carefully aiming his telescope, immediately recognised the flags swirling from the ships.

Still peering through the telescope he screamed out, 'Star and Stripes on the larboard bow!' his voice fading into the ocean.

With the telescope still extended awkwardly in one hand he blew his whistle loudly and, now joined by the lookout in the crows nest, they blew their whistles simultaneously in long extended bursts alerting the crew and waking the whole ship.

The *Raytheon* suddenly burst into life.

The crew, many still almost naked, appeared from every edifice.

'Go aloft, Jimmy!' screamed the boatswain as he struggled to pull his braces over his sweat stained vest.

'Aye, aye, sir!' replied Jimmy as he knuckled his forehead. While the remainder of the crew took their well-rehearsed positions throughout the ship, Jimmy ran towards the rigging and pulled himself effortlessly up. In the distance, the smaller of the two American ships turned and raced across the horizon and the larger USS *Libertine*, a French built ship, attempted to follow.

'Man-o-war, sir,' shouted Jimmy his voice almost inaudible except to the well-trained ears of the boatswain and the ship's captain.

Captain Jonas Sleep, an erect mature man, stood resplendent in his immaculate uniform even at that time of the morning. He was a very experienced seaman having spent most of his life on board one ship or another until he had been given command of his first ship under Nelson and then command of the much larger Raytheon.

His razor sharp mind took over.

'Alter course, Mr Hartman,' he ordered.

Isaac Hartman, the First Lieutenant repeated the Captain's instruction and the disciplined crew burst into action and scattered. Many of them climbed throughout the rigging working hard to adjust the yards of canvas. Their efforts were soon rewarded and the ship gained speed and veered towards their American adversary.

'Enemy on the same bearing, sir,' gushed Isaac Hartman excitedly.

Isaac, a rugged, blonde haired man in his mid-twenties, had served with the Captain for several years and they had built up an unusual relationship, so much so that they now lived close to each other high on the Devonshire moor overlooking the Tamar.

Captain Sleep stood proudly watching the activity going on around him and gave himself a congratulatory smile as the well-rehearsed preparations were meticulously carried out. 'Load, but do not run out, Mister Hartman,' he said slowly.

Below deck there was furious activity as the gunners prepared, loading double shot into the huge canon that lined both sides of the gun decks.

Captain Sleep followed this with more instructions in quick succession. 'Beat to quarters, Mister Harrison. Make ready for action.'

'Aye, aye, sir,' replied the master gunner as the drummers beat out a steady rhythm.

While the main deck was hurriedly stripped, the screens removed and the decks sanded, anything that couldn't be packed including any livestock, pigs and chicken, still in their coups, were reluctantly thrown into the sea.

Thomas Irwin, a well-dressed young man in his late twenties, and clearly not part of His Majesty's regular crew appeared on deck and stood close to the Captain.

His demeanour was readily apparent, twitching fingers, nervous fidgeting and his frequent furtive looks into the distance, became more exaggerated to anyone who took the time to notice him. Unable to suffer any longer he rushed away unnoticed to be violently sick. His moans and vomiting were drowned out by the incessant rattle of drums, the stampede of the seamen's feet grinding into the sanded decks as they rushed to their stations and the red coated Marines as they took up their stations in the hammock netting and high in the fighting tops.

Captain Sleep propped his eyeglass on the midshipman's shoulder and eyed their enemy.

Isaac Hartman returned to the Captain's side.

'Cleared for action, sir,' he said the nervousness clearly apparent in his voice.

The Captain raised his eyeglass and slowly nodded. 'Will they fight or run, Mister Hartman?' he asked.

His question was answered for him.

'They're running for it, sir!' screamed Jimmy.

The Captain maintained his composure. 'Trim the sails,' he ordered.

The deckhands rushed to raise the remainder of the

huge sails and as they took up the wind the *Raytheon* sliced deep into the sea. The fully rigged ship was a sight to behold and for a moment the deckhands stood in wonderment as the beautiful vessel made its way silently along the east coast of the United States.

'Turn about, Mister Hartman,' instructed Captain Sleep.

His order found its way swiftly along the deck.

'Look lively there,' boomed the boatswain to the crew high in the rigging.

While the *Raytheon* sped in the direction of the enemy, Captain Sleep once again planned his next manoeuvre.

'Now she'll fly, lads,' shouted the Captain proudly as the ship ploughed heavily into the waves.

'Aye, aye, sir,' replied Isaac Hartman grinning, clearly pleased and honoured to be one of Captain Sleep's trusted officers.

The British ship made up a great deal of ground and when she was within a few miles of the American ship Captain Sleep gave the instruction that the impatient gunners had been waiting for. 'Open the ports, run out,' he ordered. His instructions were followed instantaneously; the portholes were opened and for the first time the enemy ship could be clearly seen by the gunners.

The Captain reached across to the crewman, grabbed his eyeglass and scrutinised the decks of the enemy. He returned the eyeglass to its custodian just as quickly as he'd taken it and for the first time his face underwent a sombre transformation. He could sense the mixed feelings of anticipation and excitement sweeping throughout the vessel and as Captains had done so many times before on the numerous ships on which he had once served, he said a prayer.

'For what we are about to receive may the Lord make us truly thankful,' he said softly. He looked around at his officers and across the decks at his crew and after briefly closing his eyes he gave the instruction that they had all been waiting for. 'On the up roll, Mister Finchley,' he boomed.

He forced a reassuring smile and nodded. 'Good luck, men.'

Below deck, Thomas Irwin stood in the shadows and trembled with fear. It had been his on father's insistence that he made the hazardous journey to Nova Scotia and the idea of being involved in a sea battle had never seriously entered either of their thoughts.

The USS *Libertine* opened the firing, her first shots ploughed into the sea short of their target and as the sound of the enemy's guns boomed across the water, Thomas slid to the floor, the darkness temporarily swallowing his shrinking cowardly body. At that moment he felt as though his world was at an end.

The guns of the *Raytheon* fired more accurately and the long double-shotted eighteen pounders thundered as they returned the fire of the oncoming *Libertine*.

The shot ploughed into the American ship's main mast and rigging and the whole vessel bellowed in agony as her crew were torn apart. The uninjured crew emerged through the smoke, debris and flames to continue the fight for their very existence.

The American guns now returned more accurate fire and the *Raytheon* and her crew came under heavy bombardment from the guns loaded with chain shot - jagged pieces of iron, which tore into the top sails and ripped them to pieces. The deck hands and Marines were slowly torn apart as it ripped through the piled hammocks hurling many of the men, screaming and kicking to the opposite side of the ship.

'Take care!' screamed the midshipman, his throat already sore from gulping the dense gunpowder laden smoke. 'They're bloody well firing langridge, sir.'

Captain Sleep acknowledged the midshipman with a slow knowing nod as yet another shot hit the *Raytheon's* already perilous decking, ripping the rigging and sending timber shrapnel and burning canvas crashing down onto the already injured seamen. The burning sails dropped slowly to the deck in a perverse and beautiful motion, a stark contradiction to the impending destruction.

The midshipman hit by shards of flying metal and splinters could only stand and stare in horror as his once white breeches were splashed with blood and finely cut pieces of his fellow shipmate's skin. He swayed under the explosion and opened his mouth but all he could do was to mouth nothingness before racing aft to help others suffering the same fate.

Thomas Irwin squirmed in the shadows amid the deafening roar and acrid smoke, sweating profusely. Shaking with fear he screamed into the darkness, clearly a very desperate coward.

The guns from both ships continued to belch venom

and smoke from their decks but this time there was no double shot, time was much too precious.

Firing randomly, the two ships continued to close in on each other.

'Stop yer vents... sponge out... load... run out!' bellowed Captain Sleep, followed by a quick fire succession of desperate orders that if not timed to the second could result in yet another individual's loss of life.

Between each firing the gunners worked relentlessly to sponge and worm out the guns before firing again. If it was not done they could likely explode the next time they were fired. The regular drills had ensured they were all razor sharp. The movement was perfect, except for the occasional gun damaged by a misfire.

The only response was a continuation of the frantic activity as the gunners loaded, fired, cleaned and then repeated the process. When a gun and its gunner were hit, the men were dragged aside and replaced, and the action would start all over again. There was no time to think about what was happening around them they all had a job to do and would continue to do it until they were either badly injured, ordered to stop or were dead.

The decks ran with blood.

Injured men lay moaning where they fell, their bodies contorted and twisted amongst the burning timber and sails. The lucky ones lay dead, crushed and dismembered beneath the splintered masts, rigging and fellow crew members, while the less seriously injured managed to crawl, dragging their broken limbs along the deck.

There was no respite. In some places the blood had already dried and the dark stains resembled black tar, reflecting the bright sun as it periodically pierced the smoke and flames.

Richard Bateman, the midshipman, knelt on the bloodied deck.

'We lost Mr Harris, sir.'

Captain Sleep having had his concentration broken snapped back at him. 'What man?' he snarled.

'Mr Harris is mortally wounded, sir,' he repeated.

The Captain acknowledged Richard Bateman with a curled lip and returned to review the battle.

Whilst the crew rushed around the deck and removed some of the dead, Doctor William Fogarty, the ship's surgeon, a plump middle-aged man, awkwardly dodged the incoming shot and the ensuing debris as it flew through the air from every angle, and checked as many of the wounded as he could.

The American ship had not fared any better, its decks burned fiercely and out of control, flames spread from pockets all over the deck. Thick choking smoke filled the air and compounded the chaos. Captain Nathaniel Coombes, a handsome young man, stood on the deck and tried desperately to direct his men, while Dylan Chipp, a middle aged civilian, ripped his expensive well cut suit as he tried to dodge the incoming shot and resulting shards of timber and metal. He rushed jerkily from place to place in an attempt to find somewhere, anywhere, safe to hide. Now almost delirious and crazed with fear he rushed towards Captain Coombes.

'Captain, we're being ripped to shreds,' he screamed.

Captain Coombes had no time for civilians, he never had. 'Get him out of ma sight!' He turned his back, 'Mister Barley, release those below decks,' he shouted.

Dylan Chipp, ever the businessman, grabbed at his arm and screamed. 'You can't release the black bastards, they're my property,' he spluttered, 'mmm... worth good money.'

'What good's a dead slave? How much do you think they'll be worth then?' countered Ram Barley angrily.

Dylan Chipp didn't have time to reply, a musket ball flew close to his right ear, splitting the lobe in two. 'I've been hit,' he shrieked.

Captain Coombes ignored him and hurriedly returned to Ram Barley. 'Release them! What are yer waiting for? Get on with it, man,' he ordered.

'Aye, aye, sir' replied the midshipman as he ran along the flaming deck towards the stairs and hazardous darkness.

Below decks a group of black slaves, Miles Longman, Joshua Amos, Moses Reading and Jerome Millington, lay chained and totally defenceless in the thick smoke and heat. Their prison periodically illuminated either by the flames from the fires that broke out around them or the occasional sunlight which shot its glaring early morning rays through the damaged hull as the ship rose and fell.

Up on deck, the British guns continued to hit their target inflicting greater damage on the now defenceless Americans. Flaming sails and larger pieces of burning timber crashed around them, killing and maiming the crew and officers.

Ram Barley made his way precariously through the thick smoke and flames to unlock the chains of the four remaining slaves. They could only look on as a shot pierced the ship's hull a few feet from them blasting large pieces of wood, metal and lethal splinters of sharp timber into their bare skin, and cutting deep into their bodies. Jerome lay motionless, his skull split in two by the chain that had kept him captive for so many weeks.

Ram Barley unlocked their chains but there was no time for the terrified slaves to savour their freedom as another volley of shots hit the hull sending yet more timber and shrapnel towards their exposed and aching bodies.

'Get out of 'ere. Save yerselves if you can,' screamed Ram before disappearing into the smoke.

Miles knelt beside Jerome's lifeless body, a true friend, his only friend, and he was dead. He bent his head, resting it on Jerome's bloody chest. He stared blindly at the lifeless body of his dearest friend and sobbed uncontrollably.

'Cum on mon, he'm lang ded... le's go... 's too late, ye cun do nuttin' fer dat paw basterd,' screamed Moses.

Moses tugged at Miles, grabbed Joshua and dragged them along the deck.

The three of them made their way through the

wreckage and carnage towards the light, naively expecting it to be safer on deck.

High in the rigging William Cole aimed, fired his musket, reloaded and fired again and again in the direction of the officers on the *Raytheon*.

As Miles, Joshua and Moses Reading crept nervously onto the main deck they stood and attempted to take in the horror around them. The stench of burning flesh and gunpowder wafted through the thick heavy air, choking them as they gazed at the carnage perpetrated by the British guns.

Ram Barley barely conscious and pinned beneath a large piece of misshapen timber, now unrecognisable as a mast, moaned loudly. Miles Longman ran across the deck and effortlessly lifted the huge piece of now useless mast and tried desperately to release him. Ram winced when he saw the deep leg wound and exposed bone and as he tried to pull himself from beneath the timber a severed rib sliced through the skin of his bare chest. Miles screamed at Moses while he maintained his hold. Moses reluctantly joined him but as he dragged Ram from under the timber a piece of shrapnel cut deep into his bare back and he fell to the deck screaming as the wound spewed blood down the back of his legs and onto his bare feet.

The *Raytheon* closed in on the USS *Libertine* but despite the hopelessness the American ship refused to surrender and continued to fire haphazardly at the British ship.

Captain Sleep stood on the deck and muttered under his breath. 'Strike you bastard! <u>Strike</u>!' Gritting his teeth, he shook his head in total disbelief before whispering to himself. 'So be it.'

After slowly surveying the scene around him, he partially closed his eyes, lowered his sword and the unforgiving guns blasted away at the American ship. The heavy fire wreaked havoc and once more Captain Sleep raised his sword. 'Royal Marines stand to... fire on the up roll, Mister Bateman.' He looked across at the smoking American ship. 'Hold her steady.'

'Steady she is, sir,' replied the boatswain.

The Captain hesitated for what seemed like several long minutes before shaking his head and as he reluctantly lowered his sword he spoke through his teeth. 'Fire,' he said.

The carnage was unimaginable as the USS *Libertine*

rocked under the sheer force of the superior British gunfire killing many of the crew as the fire began to spread throughout the ship. But despite the damage the Americans continued to fire blindly.

A shot hit the deck of the *Raytheon* close to Mister Bateman. He fell to the deck wounded but after a few seconds he slowly pulled himself up and grabbed a pike, which he drove hard into the deck to hold himself unsteadily upright.

'Shorten sail and fire on the up, Mister Bateman,' screamed Captain Sleep as he raised his sword. 'Hold her steady.'

'Steady she is, sir' replied Mister Bateman, grimacing with pain.

The two ships were now within a few hundred feet of each other and Isaac Hartman mindful of the American sharpshooters strategically positioned in the rigging tried to guide his Captain out of range. 'She's struck her colours, sir!' he screamed excitedly.

There was sheer pandemonium as the news of the victory filtered to the crew throughout the ship until the celebratory cheers built to a crescendo.

'Thank God,' muttered a much relieved Captain Sleep

under his breath.

At that moment a single shot rang out from the American ship and Captain Sleep spun around and fell to the ground. Isaac Hartman looked down at his Captain and fired a glance across at the American ship and the sharpshooter.

William Cole grinned back at him as he reloaded his rifle.

'My God... Captain, you've been hit,' he said as he shook his head in total disbelief.

Captain Sleep folded with pain. 'Help me up, Mister Hartman.' He attempted to take a deep breath. 'I'm fine... only a scratch,' his voice already fading as he spoke.

Doctor Fogarty appeared on deck and took a close look at the Captain's wound.

'I need to get at that, Captain?' he said.

Captain Sleep ignored him. 'Boarding party, Mister Hartman,' he said his voice little more than a whisper.

They both looked at him their identical reaction mirrored their concern.

'I need to get that lead out and put in some stitches, Captain,' pleaded the Doctor.

Captain Sleep shrugged and made a futile attempt to pull the torn jacket around the wound.

'I'll be all right man, let's get the job done then you can do with me what you damn well like, Doctor Fogarty.' Captain Sleep looked across the deck at Mister Hartman. 'What are you waiting for man? You heard my order?'

He grabbed another breath before speaking, 'boarding party, Mister Hartman.'

'Yes, sir,' retorted Hartman as he motioned frantically to the crew.

That was all the crew needed. They let out a tumultuous yell and crowded around the gunner's mate until he opened the oak chest and handed out cutlasses, axes and pistols, which they waved excitedly in the air.

Thomas Irwin appeared from nowhere. 'Can I join them, Captain?' he asked.

The Captain gave his nodding approval. 'Look after him, Mister Hartman.'

'Aye, aye, sir,' he replied.

Thomas Irwin raced towards the chest and grabbed a pistol and cutlass from the gunner's mate.

The drummers on the poop deck played with

renewed vigour as the crew lowered a number of small craft into the Atlantic and clambered eagerly on board.

The adrenaline raced through their bodies as they rowed towards the burning beleaguered American ship screaming excitedly and shouting obscenities.

As they approached, many of the American crew, fearing for their lives, and in a futile attempt to escape capture, jumped overboard into the freezing sea.

The boatswain's eyes flitted between the seamen in the water and the Captain, 'Sir...?' he failed to finish his sentence.

Captain Sleep raised a smile, 'we'll pick them up in a few moments, we have all the time we need,' he said.

Doctor Fogarty became noticeably agitated. 'Captain....' He paused, 'if I don't get that lead out....'

The Captain gave him a reassuring tap on the shoulder, 'there's time, Doctor, there's time. Just let 'em savour the moment.' He gazed across at his men as they neared the stricken ship screaming and waving their weapons. 'Just look at them... they've earned it.' He smiled briefly then winced as the lead ball fired a painful jolt throughout his body.

The craft pulled alongside the American ship and the

British crew grappled their way on board unopposed. They were followed closely by the Marines, bayonets fixed and pointed in the direction of their captives, Isaac Hartman, other officers and finally Thomas Irwin.

'If they resist... kill 'em,' screamed Isaac Hartman.

There was no resistance from their captives who looked demoralized and stunned by what had been a bitter battle. The decks were enveloped in thick smoke and the ship rocked dangerously from side to side as the Marines took up a line behind Isaac Hartman, Thomas Irwin and a number of the more intimidating seamen.

Isaac Hartman drew his sword and took a step forward. 'This ship is a prize of war,' he said as he walked towards an exhausted and bloody Captain Coombes. 'And you... are prisoners-of-war. Officers will go first, followed by members of the crew. Bring your wounded and we will do all we can to care for them,' he said.

Dylan Chipp pushed his way to the front and the Marines immediately stiffened, pointed their rifles directly at him and pulled back the hammers.

'Who the hell are you, man?' bellowed Isaac Hartman.

'This has nothing to do with me... I'm a civilian.' He

took a huge gulp of air. 'I shouldn't be treated like them,' he bellowed.

'Take them away,' ordered Isaac. He raised his right arm and pointed firmly in the direction of Dylan Chipp. 'Him first!' he snarled.

Despite his desperate pleading and gibbering, instinctively two Marine's darted forward, grabbed him and held him in a restrained position preventing him from any movement at all.

The remaining prisoners including Miles Longman, Moses Reading, Joshua Amos and Sylas, a young boy no older than eleven, were shepherded into two groups, seamen in one group and officers in another.

Isaac Hartman reached out his hand and waited for Captain Coombes and his First Lieutenant to hand over their swords all the while looking around the deck for the sharpshooter who had wounded Captain Sleep.

Clearly shell-shocked it took a few seconds for the American Captain and his First Lieutenant to reach for their swords.

Thomas Irwin sweating profusely fiddled nervously with the hammer of his musket before he pointed it in the direction of Captain Coombes and at almost point blank range fired.

Isaac Hartman grabbed at the musket and tore it from Thomas Irwin.

Thomas shook violently, his eyes wide, white and hideous, grinning with the look of a man possessed.

'You crazy bastard!' screamed Dylan Chipp, 'what did you do that for? Didn't you see he wasn't armed? Come on kill us all! Who cares what happens to us now!'

Isaac Hartman took control. 'Get 'em moving.' He pointed to the wounded Captain Coombes. 'And get him across to the surgeon. We might be able to do something for the poor bastard.' He now turned his attention to Thomas Irwin. 'You, Mister Irwin are under arrest.' He swallowed hard. '<u>Take him away</u>!' he bawled.

An American seaman ran towards the Marines and defying their flashing bayonets, musket and rifle fire blindly threw himself overboard and disappeared beneath the burning timber and mutilated corpses of his shipmates that now littered the Atlantic.

While the prisoners-of-war were taken back to the *Raytheon*, Isaac Hartman and a handful of Marines searched what was left of the ship and identified anything they could salvage. The casks, boxes and chests were loaded onto the remaining boats before they cast off leaving the burning ship to founder out of control.

Captain Sleep stood on deck; his once immaculate uniform now soaked with his own blood gleamed scarlet in the sun. He supported himself against the solid oak rail and took in the mayhem that surrounded him watching the able bodied men as they tore at the burning sails and smoking timber and checked their crewmates for any sign of life.

The Captain pushed himself away from the rail and made his way unsteadily along deck before turning his attention to the enemy's ship as it sank slowly beneath the waves.

Jimmy nervously approached him and spoke in little more than a whisper.

'There she goes, sir....' He waited for a reaction. There was none. He continued, 'we won, sir,' he gushed innocently.

Captain Sleep forced a smile but retained his pained look. 'I know it may seem like that.' He shook his head slowly and paused before speaking. 'No one wins a war.' The Captain looked across at the American prisoners as they shuffled along the deck sandwiched between two rows of proud but battle weary Marines.

'They just lost,' he said benevolently.

Jimmy looked up at him quizzically his head tilted to one side before he turned and walked away mumbling to himself.

Below decks the gunners checked their filthy numbed bodies for wounds and gradually appreciated they at least were still alive. It had been a hard and bloody battle.

On the orlop deck, deep in the bowels of the ship, the timbers painted red so the blood stains wouldn't undermine the morale of the crew, Captain Sleep refused to be treated before his injured crew; instead he stood and waited his turn. While the ship rocked gently and the swinging lanterns created deep dark menacing shadows, the wounded were laid on old sails awaiting surgery or certain death in the stinking bloody hellhole.

The injured seaman on the makeshift operating table screamed out in pain, his only comfort a shot of rum poured into his gasping mouth by the lob lolly-boy, followed immediately by a filthy leather strap.

Doctor Fogarty, his apron stained crimson with the blood of the wounded, operated in near total darkness.

Hatred is the key

He cut into the wounded seaman's groin and using a wide bladed scarifying gouge, removed the musket ball from his misshapen body before closing the wound and turning his attention to the next patient.

Henry Wilkes lay on the operating table in severe shock, his whole body convulsed with pain. The Doctor moved closer and realizing that time was running out grasped the injured seaman's mangled left leg and sawed clumsily through it releasing a fountain of blood. His procedure complete, he threw what was left of the leg in the nearby "wings and limbs tub," straightened his back, paused briefly and shook his head in despair.

The Captain approached the dying seaman, pushed the greasy and singed hair from his eyes and stroked his powder stained forehead gently. 'You did well, Mister Wilkes,' he said.

Henry Wilkes tried to raise his head but slumped back and with his last breath spoke as he exhaled, 'he... he... he knew me name.'

The Captain caringly lowered Henry's eyelids, 'you did well.' He sighed and briefly closed his eyes in prayer before he continued. 'Let me know the bill, Doctor Fogarty,' he said softly.

Graham Sclater

ໝ Chapter two ໝ

In the moonless night, small groups of gunners and crew sat on deck and sang sea shanties, while the Marines chattered animatedly amongst themselves discussing every part of the earlier battle and their resounding victory.

The music suddenly stopped as Captain Sleep flanked by Isaac Hartman and a pained Charles Baron appeared on deck. Captain Sleep, his left arm and shoulder heavily bandaged walked awkwardly towards them. 'Another tot of rum for my most excellent crew, Mister Baron,' said the Captain as he forced a pained smile. 'You did well lads… real well,' he said with a smile.

The ship erupted and he waited patiently until the furore had subsided. 'Make a heading for Plymouth, Mister Hartman,' he said.

'Sir!' replied Isaac, his voice quivering with emotion.

'Three cheers for Captain Sleep!' shouted Charles Baron, as he waved his arms high above him.

The whole crew erupted again but this time they cheered and whistled with new found vigour.

Captain Sleep, his arm hanging awkwardly in the blood-soaked sling, sat at his oak desk and compiled his log. Isaac Hartman, followed by Thomas Irwin flanked by two Marines, knocked and entered the cabin. While Isaac stepped back into the shadows, the Marines thrust Thomas towards the Captain's desk directing him to stand to attention.

The Captain continued to write for several minutes before he stood and in obvious pain, turned his back on Thomas and the Marines. Suddenly he spun around and grim faced stared directly at Thomas. 'Well, Mister Irwin,' he stopped suddenly and nodded slowly. 'Um... I feel we have a problem,' he said.

'Problem?' queried Thomas nervously. He paused. 'Why?' he asked cockily.

'What did you say, <u>Mister</u>?' spat Captain Sleep with rage. 'And address me in the correct manner, man,' he boomed.

Thomas stiffened and for the first time he could feel

the Captain's anger. He coughed nervously. 'Um... I said I don't see why... Captain....' He coughed again. 'Sir,' he mumbled.'

'Did you realise they had lowered their colours, man?' Captain Sleep paused and subconsciously tapped his fingers on his desk until he finally slammed his fists down hard. 'They surrendered to us!' he boomed.

'Yes, Captain... but he could have killed me....'

Thomas Irwin waited for a response but there was none and twitching nervously he continued. 'Did you expect me to wait for him to put a ball in me?' he snapped.

The Captain grunted and sniggered. 'That might have been a good thing, Mister Irwin.' He tried to straighten up but the pain was too great. 'You, Mister Irwin, have blood on your hands...' his stare cutting right through him. 'You sir, will be court marshalled as soon as we reach Plymouth.'

'Court marshalled? How can that be...? I'm a civilian.' he countered.

'On my ship, Mister Irwin... you... you... will be treated like every other member of my crew,' he screamed.

Isaac Hartman smirked, nodded in agreement, looked across at the Marines and then at Thomas Irwin.

'My father won't agree to that,' spluttered Thomas.

The Captain shuffled slowly towards him and stood within a few inches of Thomas Irwin's sweating face, his lips quivering with anger. 'Didn't you hear what I said, man?' You're on board at your father's request. This is my ship and you are under my command.' He snarled. 'Do you honestly expect me to afford you special treatment?' He paused, before suddenly exploding. 'Your father has absolutely no say in how I run my ship! Do you understand that..., Mister Irwin?' He took a deep breath and a look of utter revulsion crossed his face. 'Take him away!' he screamed.

'You bastard!' screamed Thomas Irwin. 'You can't do this to me. My father will have you flogged,' he said defiantly.

Captain Sleep lowered himself awkwardly into his seat and spoke in a soft voice, 'twenty lashes....' He slowly tapped his desk with his index finger. 'Just get him out of my sight,' he said quietly.

The Marines stepped forward, grabbed Thomas and dragged him screaming out of the cabin. The Captain, his fist clenched tightly in anger, motioned to Isaac to sit.

'Take a glass with me, Mister Hartman.'

'Aye, that would be very welcome, sir... being so many miles from home, sir,' he sighed.

Captain Sleep reached across to the ornate decanter and awkwardly poured two glasses of cognac. He passed the first glass to Isaac. 'Plymouth, Mister Hartman, Plymouth,' he said quietly.

They both sipped slowly and smiled.

'In a few weeks, we'll be within sight of England, Mister Hartman,' he said, reflecting.

'To be honest with you, sir, it can't come soon enough,' said Isaac. 'What with the new baby.' He sighed. 'I wish I could have seen her....' He reflected, 'been there, sir.'

The Captain smiled broadly. 'She's probably not got her sea legs yet, Mister Hartman.' He pushed himself into his chair, deep in thought, his mind elsewhere, until he heard the muffled music, and smiled softly.

'There is still time... still time.'

Whilst many of the crew worked feverishly to repair the rigging, sails and damaged deck they stopped briefly and stood to watch as the two Marines dragged an ashen faced Thomas Irwin up onto deck. The grating was set up on end and tied against the mainmast and Thomas was stripped to the waist and lashed to it.

'The tail if you please, Mister Baron,' asked a smirking Mister Fincham.

Charles Baron passed him the torturous instrument and the Master Gunner, flexed his muscles. He cracked the cat o' nine tails on the deck and stood waiting for the signal from Captain Sleep. The Captain twitched his instruction and Thomas Irwin screamed out in agony as the first flail of the cat cut deep into his soft pale flesh.

'You have no right to do this to me, this is a grave injustice,' he cried.

In a futile attempt of compassion he turned his head to the Captain and waited for him to intervene.

Isaac Hartman looked towards his Captain but there was no reaction. 'Continue, Mister Fincham,' ordered Captain Sleep in a firm voice.

The Master Gunner pulled back the cat o' nine tails and struck out.

The crew counted loudly until all twenty lashes had been administered with great precision to the deeply lacerated and bleeding back of a now unconscious

Thomas Irwin.

Two crewmen stepped forward, cut him down and dragged him across the deck.

The wounded prisoners beneath deck, including a severely wounded and bleeding Captain Coombes, lay uncomfortably, cramped conditions shackled to each other. The ship sped towards England and away from their homeland and in the tense atmosphere they felt every wave as the ship crashed through them.

Miles Longman, Joshua Amos and Moses Reading were shackled to two white crewmen and had listened in silence to the screams of Thomas Irwin. It was strangely bizarre for them to hear a white man taking a beating rather than themselves.

'What's yer name, boy?' asked Ram Barley.

Miles Longman was thinking of his wife and young children and didn't hear him.

'You, boy,' shouted Ram, pointing directly at Miles.

Benjamin Beck nudged him and a shocked Miles jumped and attempted to stand but the chains pulled him awkwardly backwards.

'I said, what's yer name boy?' Ram Barley screwed up his face and continued, 'not too difficult a question for you is it?' he asked.

'Miles, massa,' stuttered the wounded slave. 'Miles Longman.'

'Well, Miles Longman.' A smile crossed his face and he continued in his strong southern drawl, 'I'm very pleased to have made your acquaintance... I owe you a great many thanks,' he said.

The confused slave stared back at him.

Ram Barley coughed and held his ribs before he replied. 'For saving ma life, boy,' he said.

'Tank ya, massa, I wuz doin' wha' any a dem God fearin' mon would hadda dun,' said Miles, finding it hard to hide his embarrassment.

Dylan Chipp stiffened. 'Saving your life...,' he cursed. 'What was the point of that? We're all going to die down here anyhow.' He pointed at Miles before turning to Ram Barley. 'He only postponed the day for you... you'll soon be wishin' he'd left you there. At least you'd have been at peace by now.' He slowly took in the prisoners around him. 'Just look at us,' he murmured.

Charles Francis, a middle-aged man who had spent most of his life in the Deep South became agitated. 'How comes you're talking to a nigger like that? They ain't no

Mister where I come from... them's just plain slaves... boy.' He glared across at Miles and sniggered.

'That's why he would have left <u>you</u> to die,' screamed Ram Barley. 'You should treat people with some respect and then maybe....' He lowered his voice, 'just maybe you'll get out of here alive. Who knows... perhaps in one piece?' He smirked as he leaned his head against the hull.

Not wishing to draw attention to himself, Joshua Amos nervously reached up and slowly wiped the sweat from his pock marked face.

Dylan Chipp suddenly snapped. 'Just let me out of here,' he screamed. 'I shouldn't be down here with these bastards. I'm not a fighter,' he said angrily.

Peter Beck, Benjamin's older brother, straightened his wire rimmed spectacles and spoke out. 'Who cares? You're stuck with us for the duration, Mister Chipp, sir, and I would suggest you get used to your newly discovered world.'

While they sniggered loudly the American Captain moaned in pain and tried to move but slumped back unconscious.

The crewmen dragged a semi-conscious Thomas Irwin towards them and dropped him heavily to bleed into the deck.

Dylan Chipp suddenly became agitated and screamed at them. 'Can't you get me out of here? This war has nothing to do with me!'

The nearest crewman moved unexpectedly and hit Dylan across the head causing his split lobe to reopen and spew blood everywhere. The crewman grabbed at Dylan's hair and twisted his head in the direction of Thomas Irwin. 'Shut up or you'll be flogged like 'im.' He laughed loudly and walked away.

In the darkness Captain Coombes took one last breath and died.

The next morning the crew and American prisoners assembled on deck and a handful of them nervously laid the body of Captain Coombes on a plank and draped it with the American flag. Captain Sleep said a few words, the plank was tilted and the body slid silently in to the sea. The American prisoners couldn't hide their emotion any longer and as they wiped their eyes they turned their anger in the direction of the shamefaced Thomas Irwin.

'Cold blooded murderer!' shouted Dylan Chipp.

As the anger began to grow amongst the American prisoners they suddenly began to chant in unison.

'Murderer... murderer... murderer!' they screamed.

Fearing for his life Thomas Irwin let out a tormented scream that echoed across the vast expanse of ocean.

Captain Sleep, a seasoned campaigner of many battles, knew it could so easily have been him, swallowed hard. 'Back to your stations, men,' he ordered.

'Aye aye, sir... let's get some more sail on her,' yelled Isaac Hartman as he carefully folded up the flag and passed it to one of the American prisoners who tucked it surreptitiously inside his shirt.

While the crew rushed around the deck and climbed up into the rigging, carrying out repairs, Dylan Chipp sidled up to Captain Sleep. 'Captain, I'm rich. Can't you release me at the nearest port?' He began to sweat profusely as desperation got the better of him. 'I'm rich... I... I... shouldn't be here.... He looked around shook his head and continued. 'I'm a civilian.' He lowered his voice to a whisper, 'I'll make it worth your while.'

Captain Sleep looked across to him, 'What are you saying, man? Don't you know we're at war? You were on the ship of our enemy.'

Dylan stuttered, 'well yes... but I'm not....' He inhaled deeply, 'this goddamn war's nothing to do with me.'

'Take 'im away, Mister Hartman,' the Captain boomed.

'Clap the impudent beggar in chains until we dock in Plymouth.'

'You heard the Captain. Take him away,' ordered Isaac Hartman.

A trio of Marines immediately grabbed Dylan and marched him across the deck screaming, before dragging him below.

The sky that had been clear an hour earlier gave way to dark heavy rain laden clouds and within minutes the strong westerly wind whipped up the sea sending huge waves crashing across the decks.

Deep in the bowels of the ship Doctor Fogarty struggled to keep awake as he worked and tried to administer some semblance of medical treatment to the dozens of injured men who still continued to moan and cry out in pain. He couldn't fail to notice that the extreme roll of the ship now made use of the makeshift operating table extremely precarious.

The Captain was taking a well earned rest in his cabin when Charles Baron knocked and entered, such informality having been previously agreed due to the Captain's injury.

'Captain Sleep, sir, storm up ahead.' He cleared his throat. 'Looks like a bad one, sir,' he said.

'You know what to do,' replied the Captain taking a breath before continuing. 'I'll be up to join you shortly,' he replied in a pained voice.

'Yessir!' said Charles Baron as he rushed through the still open door.

The ship listed heavily and below deck in almost total darkness the prisoners nervously awaited the impending storm. Dylan Chipp shook and nervously chewed at his fingers. He suddenly snapped and cried out. 'We're all gonna die! Guards! Guards!' He waited for a reaction, there was none. With that, a surge of gushing ice cold sea crashed over him and the other prisoners. 'At least give us some sort of chance,' he spluttered.

The ship began to take on water as the now gigantic waves crashed across the decks. Battered by heavy rain and the storm force winds the crew high in the rigging fought to gather and tie the sails.

Captain Sleep, his cloak wrapped loosely around him and still in great pain, clung on to the bridge with one hand.

The boatswain shouted up to him, 'we'm gonna need some more 'elp 'ere, Captain.' He was immediately swamped by a huge wave and shook his head before he continued. 'That is if we'm gonna 'ave any chance of gettin' thro' this un.'

'Mister Hartman, bring up the prisoners,' said the Captain. He deliberated before he continued, 'no... only the able bodied men. I don't wish to lose any more of 'em.' He motioned to the boatswain, 'you help him, Mister.'

'Aye aye, sir,' replied the boatswain proudly.

The fittest of the American prisoners made their way on deck followed by a terrified Dylan Chipp who upon seeing the huge waves shook violently. 'What do you expect me to do?' he chattered with absolute fear.

'Take the rope and lash down the sail,' screamed Peter Beck.

Dylan made his way towards the flapping sail but a fierce gust of wind caught him and he was dragged along the deck and over the side. He screamed out with pain as the rope cut into his soft hands. Moses Reading slid along the deck and after tying a rope around his waist effortlessly pulled Dylan back onto deck. He reached inside his boot, removed a knife and cut a much relieved Dylan Chipp free. His relief was short lived as the storm reached its peak and a loose piece of timber, damaged in the battle and not yet replaced, crashed down beside him and the torn sails flapped deafeningly around him.

Dylan, whimpering with shock ran below deck to examine his heavily bleeding and painful hands.

Captain Sleep moved closer to Isaac Hartman. 'We've done all we can, Mister Hartman.' He struggled to speak as the gale took his breath away. 'Just pray she blows herself out,' he mouthed.

'Yessir,' he replied, pulling his cape tightly around his drenched uniform.

Throughout the night the damaged ship was at the mercy of the storm and at first light Captain Sleep and his crew surveyed the damage. The sails were carefully examined and those still in good order were carefully hoisted up the makeshift rigging and while other members of the crew cleared the debris from the decks, the carpenters carried out repairs to the masts.

'I reckon we've been extremely lucky, Mister Hartman,' said a pale and exhausted Captain as he looked out on to a calm sea. 'How is it she be so evil one day and a beauty to behold the next, eh Mister Hartman?'

Isaac sighed heavily and slowly nodded his agreement.

The American prisoners under the surveillance of the Marines walked slowly onto a section of the cleared deck and nodded thankfully up to the Captain, who bowed his head in recognition of their gratitude.

A flock of gulls circled the ship squawking excitedly. Captain Sleep looked up at them and smiled. 'We are close to the end of what has been a very torturous journey, Mister Hartman,' he said thankfully.

The crew cheered loudly but the American prisoners were unable to share their excitement or to hide their fear of what lay ahead.

Hatred is the key

෨෨෬

෨ඏ **Chapter three** ෨ඏ

The gleaming barouche carrying Judith Sleep, Rachel
Hartman and Emily rattled its way across the moor and
down into Yelverton, past clusters of stone cottages and
through Plymouth towards the dock.

'I trust Isaac will love Emily,' asked Rachel nervously.

'Why shouldn't he? She's absolutely beautiful, a credit
to you both,' said Judith. 'I wish we had had children,'
she said looking sad. 'But the Captain didn't seem to
have interest in them.' She glanced briefly across at little
Emily, smiled and then gazed longingly out of the
window.

The damaged *Raytheon* limped slowly along the Devon
coast, into Plymouth Sound, up the Hamoaze and into
the River Tamar passing dilapidated hulks *El Firm*, *Le
Caton*, *Genereux*, *Ganges*, *Vanguard* and *Europe*, now all

used as prison ships. It moored temporarily alongside the *Le Brave*, the HQ of Prison Ships, and Captain Edward Hawkins, Superintendent of Prisons and Prison ships, boarded with his Marines.

He was greeted by a very relieved Captain Sleep who handed him a list of prisoners-of-war.

'A tough campaign, Captain Sleep?' he asked.

The Captain looked directly at him and grinned. 'You could say that, Captain,' he said his face haggard and pained.

Captain Hawkins looked across at the prisoners, smiled a broad smile and licked his lips. 'We'll take care of 'em now, Captain.' He paused. 'Your work is done.'

A group of hardened militia from the Shropshire Regiment waited impatiently for the Americans to disembark and as their charges left the *Raytheon* for the last time they herded them onto the filthy, stinking deck of the *San Pareil*. The Spanish ship was captured off Ferrol in 1805 and had been used as a prison ship in the Tamar since 1810.

'Let's be 'avin' yer!' yelled the first militiaman, as he jabbed his bayonet forcefully into Dylan Chipp's fat belly.

'Get a move on or you'll feel <u>me</u> <u>steel</u>!' yelled another.

Dylan Chipp shook his head, 'Coombes was such a lucky bastard,' he said, moaning as he staunched the bleeding.

The prisoners-of-war were processed and any marks or scars were carefully examined and the information documented before they were issued with a hammock, a straw filled palliasse, a bolster, blanket, jacket, waistcoat, trousers, shirt, shoes, stockings and a handkerchief.

Again Dylan Chipp complained profusely accepting only a hammock and bedding and choosing to wear his own ripped and bloodied suit, stockings and shoes.

On the quayside there was understandable excitement as the families waited to welcome their loved ones. The screams, of those saddened by the news that their loved ones would not be returning home, were muted by the whoops of delight from the lucky ones.

Traders mixed with the crowd and street sellers touted hot chestnuts, freshly baked bread and seafood while fire eaters and jugglers performed to a captive audience.

Squire Robert Irwin impeccably dressed but clearly overweight stood proudly waiting for his son. Close by Judith Sleep and Rachel Hartman with baby Emily waited in anticipation for their husbands. They had received correspondence a week earlier and knew their husbands would be returning safely but Captain Sleep had kept the letter brief giving no indication of his injuries.

The *Raytheon* glided into the Sound and tied up alongside the Barbican quay. The same quay that had seen the Pilgrim Fathers leave England aboard the Mayflower for the New World on 6th of September 1620.

'C'mon lads, let's drink Plymouth dry,' shouted the boatswain. 'The quicker we put the sails to bed the quicker we get ashore.'

'Yes, sir!' shouted the crew in unison.

Thomas Irwin tried to straighten his twisted and aching body but, still in obvious pain, set foot awkwardly onto the quayside and shuffled apprehensively towards his father.

'What's the matter with you, son?' asked Squire Irwin. 'Are you wounded? Have you seen action?' he asked anxiously.

'Sir, I had an accident,' replied Thomas flinching nervously.

'Accident...? What sort of accident?' enquired the

Squire, spluttering with rage.

Thomas shook his head and continued to stare at the floor. 'Take me away from <u>him!</u>' he mumbled. He pointed across to Captain Sleep who ably assisted by Charles Baron and Isaac Hartman made his way uncertainly along the quay.

Judith Sleep ran across to her husband. 'Are you all right?' she asked fearfully.

Captain Sleep kissed her softly on the forehead. 'I'll be fine...,' he murmured trying to reassure her but she shook uncontrollably. He continued in a tired voice. 'Rest... I just need some rest that's all.'

Squire Irwin pushed his way through the crowd and made his way towards Captain Sleep. 'Sir, what have you done to my son?' he cried.

Isaac Hartman pushed him aside. 'Let me help you, Captain,' he pleaded and with the help of Charles Baron and two of his crew bundled him unceremoniously into the carriage.

Judith stared at him in disbelief.

'Never mind,' said Captain Sleep as he shook his head slowly. 'The young....' His voiced faded as he winced in pain.

'Let's go home,' he said softly.

Isaac joined Judith, Rachel, Emily and the Captain in their carriage, leaving mayhem and waves of mixed emotions behind as the good and sad news filtered slowly through the crowded quayside.

The barouche made its way across the moor and the occupants sat in a strange silence until it stopped outside the converted longhouse that was now Isaac's home.

'Goodbye, Isaac,' said Judith. She looked across at her husband and then turned to Isaac.

'Goodbye, Mrs Sleep,' said Isaac, before turning to the Captain. 'Get some rest, Captain,' he paused and gently touched his Captain's arm. 'I shouldn't give any heed to that matter, sir.'

Mrs Sleep smiled. 'Thank you,' she mouthed.

The Captain nodded and waved the driver on.

The carriage made its way across the moor and travelled for nearly an hour before driving beneath an impressive carved granite arch and turning into a long gravel drive.

An Irish wolfhound appeared from nowhere and instinctively knowing his master was on board chased excitedly after the carriage until it reached the family home.

The vast estate of Bellever Park covered more than three hundred and twenty acres of moorland and was within reach of Ashburton, Plymouth and Tavistock. The estate was considered to be one of the most prestigious properties on the moor. His prize money had been substantial and Captain Sleep decided to construct the stylish property he had constantly dreamed of during his many years at sea.

The Captain had his home designed by an Exeter architect based on a property he had frequented in the West Indies and although that had been constructed of timber, due to the location and availability of materials, his Dartmoor residence was built from local granite with timber from the best Devonshire forests.

The carriage pulled to a halt immediately in front of the imposing main entrance and the Captain and his wife were welcomed by their members of staff who stood apprehensively on the wide granite steps.

The driver opened the door of the barouche and nodded. 'Welcome home, sir,' he said with a smile.

The Captain and his wife were helped out of the coach by their welcoming servants. He reached out and stroked the dog but his pained face clearly displayed the agony he was going through.

He entered the hall and after pausing for a minute to take in his surroundings, he smiled to himself before he climbed the wide staircase to his bed chamber, ably assisted by his servants.

The Captain dropped gently onto his bed and immediately fell asleep. The servants carefully covered him with several blankets and a thick eiderdown.

'Will that be all, sir?' said one servant in a low voice.

There was no reply.

The open fire blazed in the master bed chamber and as Judith carefully removed the blood sodden bandages from her husband she drew her head back in alarm at the foul smell of rotting flesh. 'This is very badly infected Jonas, we need to do something about it or I fear you will lose your arm,' she said.

The Captain looked up at her. 'So be it,' he said softly.

A young woman in her early twenties, and the much older hunchbacked man, entered the impressive hall. They acknowledged Mrs Sleep with a knowing nod before they followed her in silence up the heavily carved sweeping staircase. They stared in awe at the sheer size of the vast oil paintings of beautiful naval ships, sea battles and Captain Sleep's nautical ancestors that filled the walls. They stopped on the half landing and gazed up at the painting of Horatio Nelson carefully positioned to look down on everyone who climbed the imposing staircase. The hunchbacked man nodded with pride before continuing to the landing where Mrs Sleep guided them to the door of the master bed chamber.

They entered the sun drenched room and acknowledged the Captain with a slow knowing nod. The man placed the snakeskin bag on a table beside the bed while the woman carefully removed the soiled linen from the Captain's shoulder and chest. They stood back reflecting before the woman proceeded to remove a jar from the bag and with great precision placed a handful of maggots directly onto the gaping gangrenous wound. She mentally noted the position of the shadow on the wall and nodded to the man.

While the maggots gorged on the rotting flesh and cleaned the wound the man sat and waited patiently, looking first around the large beautifully furnished room before he stood and moved towards the huge bay window and gazed out across the moor.

The woman re-checked the position of the shadow on the wall, walked across to the bed, removed the maggots, examined the wound and gave a congratulatory smile to the man and Mrs Sleep. The man removed a glass phial containing an orange liquid and passed it to the woman who dripped it carefully onto the wound, covered it with sphagnum moss, and applied a new dressing.

''Ee should feel betta zun, madam,' she said as she closed the bag.

She finally looked up at Mrs Sleep and spoke in a soft voice. ''Ee be very lucky man, looks like the ball missed 'is lung be less dan inch. 'Ee needs as much rest as possible and ee'll be right as rain 'gin,' she said with a confident smile.

The man picked up the bag and they made their way towards the bedroom door.

'Thank you,' said Judith as she looked across at her husband. 'Thank you very much,' she said softly.

She pulled the crisp white sheets over her husband's shoulders and tiptoed out of the room.

Moans and groans filled the toxic air as the American prisoners dragged their naked and swollen feet along the cramped, dark, stinking lower deck, putrid water and urine dripping onto them as they searched for the impossible clean, dry space.

'If they keep us down 'ere for long we're all going to die,' said an overwhelmed Peter Beck.

'They'll soon have me out. My partners won't leave me here to rot,' said Dylan with a wry smile.

A prisoner deep in the darkness laughed loudly and coughed. 'Once they shove you in 'ere no one cares if ya lives or dies,' he said.

'They will!' screamed Dylan in denial.

'We'm all equal in 'ere,' shouted another.

'Yeah, that's as maybe but I am!' he fumed. 'In New Orleans everyone knows, Dylan Chipp.'

'Well then... why is you still 'ere?' asked the invisible mocking stranger.

The slaves looked on in silence.

Protected from the cold wind and warmed by the bright sun Captain Sleep sat in the conservatory smoking his longpipe. He was surrounded by the huge palms and exotic flowering plants he had collected during his numerous overseas campaigns.

His dog rushed in, followed by Judith carrying a

highly decorated teapot, and matching cups and saucers on a silver tray.

'You seem so much better today, Joshua,' said Judith with a smile.

The Captain gently patted his dog and nodded slowly. 'Yes my dear, I do.' He looked around the room and took in his surroundings before he continued. 'It's been so wonderful to sleep in a real bed for the past weeks.'

While Judith poured the tea, he gazed across the moor and smiled to himself. He couldn't resist the dramatic view of the nearby Tor jutting up like a huge precious stone towards the clear blue sky and the sparkling stream in the valley below. He watched as a timid deer made its way cautiously onto the gravel at the waters edge and looked furtively in every direction before bending to drink the clear slow flowing water.

A number of Marines and militiamen walked menacingly out of the shadows. 'Come on let's 'ave 'ee. You be leavin' us,' screamed one of them.

Dylan Chipp got awkwardly to his feet, his ulcerated legs weak from the long weeks of inactivity below deck. 'I told you I'd be out of here.' He said forcing a smile.

'My friends haven't forgotten me after all,' he said, bragging arrogantly as he attempted to straighten his filthy jacket.

The other prisoners slowly helped each other to stand and cowered nervously together in groups.

The guards kicked out at several of them. 'Not you! Stay where you are! You ain't goin' nowhere!' they screamed.

One of them fell awkwardly on the deck and sniggered at those standing. 'If I was you I wouldn't be smiling.' He spat at them. 'If you fink this is bad...,' his grin broadened, 'then you's just wait.'

'Bring yer hammocks and follow me,' ordered the Marine Sergeant.

Before any of them could ask why, they were shepherded towards the light.

'Move along there... you Yankee bastards,' screamed the Militiaman.

Peter and Benjamin Beck, Miles Longman, Moses Reading, Joshua Amos, Ram Barley, Charles Francis, Dylan Chipp and Sylas, the young boy, along with a number of other prisoners were marched along the deck passing hundreds of very sick and dying prisoners-of-war.

As they made their way up onto the slimy rotten deck the sun temporarily blinded them and for the first time they were able to gaze at the green rolling hills of Devonshire. A feeling of euphoria took over as they were each handed their daily allowance of bread and fish.

Nothing could be as bad as the hellhole they'd lived in for the past few weeks.

ക്കര

෨ℭ Chapter four ෨ℭ

The extended entourage of two hundred American prisoners-of-war, guarded by a similar number of militiamen, Marines and mounted guards, made its way out of the docks. They were soon out of Plymouth and after turning onto the new road at the *Rock* they had more than fifteen miles to walk until they reached their destination.

The prisoners, in their newly issued shoes, walked uncomfortably along the dirt road until they began to climb up onto the moor. They smiled with relief and broke into song as they looked back at the run of the Tamar and the hulks that had been their home for the past weeks.

Peter Beck cleaned his glasses, with his new handkerchief and, after replacing them, tilted his head back and took a deep breath. 'This is some beautiful place,' he said.

Benjamin took an equally deep breath and spoke as he exhaled. 'It sure is,' he replied in a much relieved voice.

Joshua and Dylan took up the rear, shackled together to the cart which carried everyone's meagre belongings and the young boy, Sylas, who had been permitted to travel in style.

Dylan coughed deeply and then shook his head in disgust. 'I just don't believe what they're doing to me,' he screamed. 'And shackled to my *own* slave!' his voice cracking in anger.

'Shut up!' screamed the nearest militiaman, as he spiked him with his bayonet. 'Keep walkin' we don't 'ave no slaves 'ere in England,' he said proudly.

'But we got prisoners,' laughed a guard.

'Thousand's of 'em,' laughed another.

The going became more difficult as the precarious uneven track and the sharp rocky outcrops broke through the heather and gorse, plentiful in the acid rich soil, cutting deep into their legs and ankles.

They stopped briefly beside a clapper bridge to eat

their meagre rations of fish and bread, resting amongst the tall fern sheaves that waved gently in the late summer breeze.

A sparrow hawk cruised above the hedge-tops before diving suddenly to ensnare a skylark.

'He's some lucky bastard,' mumbled Peter Beck, as he watched the hawk fly off into the distance with its prey.

The exhausted prisoners-of-war stopped to rest in the last valley before the moorland was to rise high above them. They sat and gazed at the crystal clear stream as it ran silently over the rocks and down towards the Tamar and Dart.

Suddenly feeling thirsty, Ram Barley stood up. 'I need a drink,' he shouted.

The Marine pointed towards the stream. 'Drink that!' he ordered.

Ram made a move towards the stream but forgot that he was shackled to Peter Beck and was jolted backwards. 'Come on, man,' he cursed.

Peter Beck slowly got to his feet and they shuffled awkwardly towards the stream.

Ram Barley knelt down, and cupping his dry hands, thrust them deep into the water before gulping it down his parched throat. He looked across at the Marines. 'Tastes like heaven after that foul smelling piss on the hulk,' he exclaimed smugly.

He leant forward again and this time plunged his head deep into the freezing water and shook it with pleasure. It was short lived as his body reacted to the cold and he shivered uncontrollably.

Smiling to himself, the Sergeant climbed back on his horse. His face suddenly changed. 'On yer feet!' he ordered. 'That is, if you don't wanna spend the night out 'ere.'

High on the moor Harold Thomson, a well built man, his long hair tied back in a ponytail, worked inside the open building smelting the tin ore. The bellows blew noisily into the furnace fanning the flames while the water wheel turned slowly powered by the stream, which ran immediately alongside the single storey granite building.

While one labourer broke down the larger stones, another labourer cracked at the smaller stones with a heavy iron stamp, and another two sieved the small pieces in the shallow stream.

The sweat ran down Harold Thomson's heavily muscled arms and shoulders as he poured the molten tin from the vat into the large moulds held by the labourers. Sensing the impending darkness he stopped what he was doing and rushed out into the farmyard. He looked towards the Tor. 'Get them animals in,' he shouted. 'There's a storm brewing,' he said confidently.

His teenage daughters, Henrietta and Alex, heeded his instruction and chased the sheep towards the barn, while their dogs yapped excitedly at their heels.

The eldest, Henrietta, who had recently celebrated her nineteenth birthday, pulled at her much younger sister. 'Come on Alex... give me a hand will yer? You knows I can't do this on me own,' she said as she stretched out and closed the wooden gates to the pen.

The sun was suddenly obliterated by thick clouds rolling off the hills and within minutes a thick fog descended enveloping them and everything on the moor.

The temperature fell dramatically and the prisoners-of-war were soon shivering. The cold began to bite into their bones and a sombre mood took hold as they realised they had been cheated.

'Get a move on!' screamed a Marine. 'That is unless you wanna be lost in this Godforsaken place,' shouted a mounted guard now invisible in the dense fog.

Hatred is the key

In the darkness they stumbled and tripped as they desperately tried to continue along the potholed track.

Suddenly they heard blood curdling screams and a pathetic figure dressed in a torn yellow uniform appeared from nowhere. *'Au secours... Au secours!'* screamed the terrified stranger in a ghastly high pitched voice. But before he could utter another word he disappeared back into the fog.

The stunned column ground to a halt and without any warning a pack of more than a dozen crazed hunting hounds rushed past them in pursuit of the Frenchman. A grey horse of some seventeen hands carrying a bearded giant of a man raced out of the fog and thundered towards them veering off at the last minute in the direction of his prey.

'Get out of my way, scum!' bawled the rider as he passed them, whipping his horse indiscriminately.

The militiamen acknowledged the rider and cheered excitedly until a few minutes later the ear piercing and blood curdling screams of the hunted man and yapping dogs confirmed they had caught their quarry and were tearing him apart.

The prisoners, shocked by what they had witnessed

suddenly broke rank.

'Get back in line!' screamed the Marines.

They began firing indiscriminately; their rifles lowered as they jabbed their bayonets threateningly towards the prisoners puncturing their exposed skin. The prisoners' anguish was compounded by an earth-shattering crack of thunder immediately above them accompanied by torrential rain which hammered their already weak and exhausted bodies.

Thick mud now engulfed their useless footwear and their meagre clothes clung to their freezing bodies.

Dylan Chipp was the first to speak. 'Can I have these off?' he pleaded, pointing to the manacles that attached him to Miles Longman.

'Keep walkin' or you'll be flogged,' screamed one of the Marines, taking in an unwelcome mouthful of rain. He struck out blindly at Miles knocking him to the ground.

'Fer sure, dis 'as ta be 'ell itself,' mumbled Miles.

'Shut up or I'll 'ave you too,' screamed the same Marine.

With every step more difficult than the last they continued their pained climb ever higher across the hostile and foreboding moor. Their frozen bones and bodies ached and the blood which had run from their cut feet congealed with the thick mud the excruciating pain making it nigh on impossible to continue walking. The fierce and incessant jabs from their captors' bayonets coerced them into summoning what little strength they had to continue.

As they neared the end of their hellish journey the rain stopped and they had their first glimpse of the exposed grey granite buildings of the Dartmoor depot. The surreal circular building jutted out of the mist and stood like an island in what was without doubt the most desolate and wild land any of them had ever seen.

It was like that in 1783, and as far as young Thomas Tyrwhitt and his companion could see through the freezing rain and low cloud, there was nothing or no living soul for miles.

The granite plateau and towering granite outcrops that was Dartmoor rose to dominate the centre of Devonshire up to 2,000 feet above sea level in what was an area of sheer desolation for much of the year.

The riders followed the pack-horse track, crossing the clapper bridges at Two Bridges and up the long sloping track through the barren and inhospitable wasteland to what was to become the start Thomas Tyrwhitt's vision.

The young traveller's vision was somewhat foolhardy, orange groves, orchards and beautiful gardens, well-fed cattle roaming and grazing on the lush grasslands and wagon loads of corn and flax being transported down to Plymouth and Tavistock. A far cry from what was a scattered land of Bronze Age settlements, burial grounds and remains of Iron Age forts, which skirted the moor.

Undeterred, Thomas, in the enviable position of secretary to the Prince of Wales, soon realised the first part of his dream when an Act of Parliament was passed to construct a road for wheeled traffic from Moretonhampstead to Tavistock.

By 1785, Thomas Tyrwhitt, at the tender age of twenty three, laid out the site for his farm at Tor Royal, a large distinctive building with its domed lead covered roof.

At the same time he built a number of moorland cottages, Miller's House at Trena Bridge alongside the Blackbrook River, and an inn, the Plume of Feathers, to accommodate many of his workers while they worked on Tor Royal. The designs of these properties closely resembled buildings he had seen on his travels to Russia but were modified to suit the exposed windswept area.

Desperate to fulfill his dreams, Thomas spent a small fortune in the area culminating in him naming the new moorland town Prince's Town after his Royal patron.

His plan foundered until 1803 when England, once again at war with France, resulted in huge numbers of French prisoners-of-war being transported back to the Tamar. Housing so many prisoners on the floating hulks in such close proximity to Plymouth posed a major threat to the nearby naval dockyards and arsenals for the Transport Board, who were responsible for all prisoners-of-war. Some were transported to the decrepit Mill Prison in Plymouth but the situation was close to breaking point.

It was not until two years later following an inspection of the proposed site at Prince's Town by members of the Transport Board that an Act of Parliament transferring the land for construction of the Dartmoor depot was tabled. It was never ratified, instead a ninety-nine year lease was agreed.

Architect Daniel Asher Alexander, renowned designer of London Dock, visited Dartmoor and together with Thomas Tyrwhitt chose the south facing slopes of

North Hessary Tor, a site conveniently near to Tor Royal. The hamlet initially known as Prince's Town was immediately renamed Princetown.

Works to build the depot were commissioned by the Transport Board, a sub-department of the Admiralty, who was deemed responsible for prisoners-of-war, the wounded and sick.

Construction of the depot commenced on 20 March 1806 when the first stone was laid by the now knighted Sir Thomas Tyrwhitt.

Initially five prison blocks were constructed within the Dartmoor depots own grounds of approximately 30 acres but, due to the high number of Napoleonic prisoners, in 1814 a further two blocks were built by the French inmates. Each block had two floors with strategically placed cast-iron pillars to support the large roof timbers for the prisoners to hang their hammocks. The newer blocks had a third floor built into the roof or cockloft with a wooden floor which was intended as exercise space in severe weather. However, due to the high number of inmates, the space was soon used to accommodate prisoners.

All the walls and buildings within it were constructed

from local granite quarried from the nearby Herne Hole quarry, transported on carts and towed by horses across the site on makeshift metal tracks.

The circular external wall constructed of huge granite blocks towering some eighteen feet above the ground concealed a road of almost a mile long where the guards and militia could move unhindered around the perimeter. A further internal wall fifteen foot high was constructed thirty foot inside the outer wall while in front of that was the third deterrent, a metal palisade some twelve foot high which surrounded the seven prison blocks along with a series of trip wires linked to alarm bells.

Platforms manned by sentries and sharpshooters were strategically positioned high on the inner wall giving them total command of the prison without making direct contact with any of the prisoners-of-war.

All the water needed for the depot was supplied from a reservoir outside the prison which in turn was fed into a round water tower near the front gates. The supply was then released into five leats which ran down the length of the prison to be used by everyone to wash themselves, their clothes, their food and to drink. The filthy foul smelling water left the prison and onto the land of Sir Thomas Tyrwhitt where it was used as fertilizer for his estate.

The Agent's residence and office, guard house, barracks, infirmary, kitchens and associated buildings were situated in various locations around the depot.

The bewildered Americans made no attempt to communicate with each other as they trudged in silence down Plymouth Hill and past the Plume of Feathers Inn before being forcibly directed to turn left into the central square in front of the Duchy Hotel. A number of off duty guards sheltering beneath the portico smoked their long pipes and watched in knowing silence as the small group of villagers stood jeering at the pathetic sight of disheartened and broken Americans as they ploughed their way through the deep muddy furrows of the rain sodden ground.

Some of the younger children rushed forward and taunted them until one of the women ran out and dragged her little boy back. 'I told 'ee before, come away from them evil Yankees,' she jeered. The crowd joined her and shouted obscenities at the prisoners. Another woman reached into her apron pocket and fingered a jagged piece of granite before throwing it at Benjamin Beck striking him on the side of the head.

He was too numb to feel it.

෧෩

∞∞ Chapter five ∞∞

The bedraggled group made its way in silence under the carved granite arched lintol. They stopped briefly to look up at the inscription *Parcere Subjectis* chiselled in the lintol above them but had no idea what it meant, before the huge metal gates slowly opened and for the first time they could see the conditions in which they would be incarcerated.

'Let's have yer. Stand to attention,' screamed Sergeant Greaves, a heavily muscled man who smirked at them as he menacingly fingered his bull whip.

It started to rain, a freezing rain.

It was hard for any of them to stand unaided let alone to attention. Instead they slouched and leaned awkwardly against one another for assistance and warmth, as they shivered.

The horse and rider made their way between the gates and stood in front of the Americans as the rain streamed from the rider's leather hat and full length deer hide overcoat and cape. The horse, covered in a combination of blood and thick mud, stood sweating and fatigued surrounded by the equally exhausted dogs who continued to bark and run excitedly around their master.

'Bloody hell,' whispered Charles Francis.

'Put 'em away!' ordered the rider.

Several of the militia jumped to attention and dragged the dogs away.

'What a mean looking bastard,' muttered William Cole.

The Sergeant cracked his whip and it wrapped tightly around the top of William Cole's arm.

'Shut up and listen!' bellowed Sergeant Greaves as he ran his hand slowly across his shaved head, stroking the imaginary hair.

William Cole could feel the blood running down his arm but was too frightened to move.

The rider moved close to the prisoners and pushed back his hat. 'Welcome to Dartmoor depot,' he said slowly. 'My name is Captain Shortland. I'm the Agent, employed by the Transport Board, and while you are here *you* will do everything *I* say... and... *my* men tell you....' He stopped and waited for a reaction. There was none. 'Sergeant Greaves will issue you with a number which will enable us to identify you. It is to be used at all times,' he boomed.

Sergeant Greaves nodded slowly and grinned at each of them, his eyes cutting into their very souls.

In the second row Peter Beck moulded his mouth and an almost inaudible high pitched sound emanated from his mouth. The Agent's mount began to kick nervously at the mud as his rider tried hard to control it.

There was an extended silence before the rider spoke.

'Some of you may have already considered escape but let me tell you this.' He paused and smiled a wry smile. 'You can try.' He paused again and waited. 'But if you did see the Frenchie today... then let me tell you, he escaped from the depot.' He looked at Sergeant Greaves and thrust his head back. 'But now he's dead,' he said with perverse pride.

Sergeant Greaves and the militiamen laughed loudly.

The rider nodded and waited as though he had done it many times before. 'And let me tell you this. If my dogs don't get you then the moor will,' he said. He pulled a cigar from his waistcoat pocket, bit off the end, spat it in the direction of the Americans and took his time to light it. He looked around at Sergeant Greaves and the militia and smirked. 'If my dogs get to you first I can promise you a quick death,' he paused and took a huge drag on the cigar and he continued to talk through the smoke. 'However it's not painless.' He took another deep drag and exhaled slowly. 'But if you die on the moor....' He lowered his voice. 'Trust me... it will be a slow agonizing death,' he sniggered.

Peter Beck lowered his head and his contorted lips created the high pitched sound again and this time the horse reared wildly and launched the Agent into the air and sent him crashing into the thick mud.

While the prisoners-of-war broke into uncontrollable raucous laughter, Sergeant Greaves and a handful of the militiamen rushed forward to help him up.

'Get away from me!' screamed the Agent with rage.

While he got unceremoniously to his feet he glared at the grinning Americans. 'If you think that was amusing let's see who has the last laugh.' He swung his muddied coat across his shoulders. 'You <u>Yankee bastards</u>!' he screamed and breathed hard before continuing, '...will stay in the yard until I find who is responsible.'

As the thick freezing mist descended around them the prisoners looked at each other in horror their faces illuminated by the handful of oil lamps hanging from the walls.

'If there is the least sign of trouble from any of these vermin... flog 'em and throw 'em in the *cachot!*' raged the Captain.

'Yessir,' replied Sergeant Greaves as he flexed his muscles and cracked his whip.

Captain Shortland looked down at his distorted cigar still smoking in the mud and kicked out furiously before he made his way to his office.

The prisoners huddled together in a futile attempt to keep warm. Ram Barley moaned, his injuries compounded by the long walk and freezing cold as the mist moved mysteriously around the yard. 'That was some awesome trick there boy,' said Ram Barley.

'Trick, call that a trick? It was suicide. If it weren't for that sonofabitch we wouldn't be sitting here in this shit now,' fumed Dylan Chipp.

'Shut up!' shouted Ram as he turned to Peter Beck.

'Tell me. Where did you learn to do that?' he asked.

'Back in Kentucky,' replied Peter timidly. He cleaned the drizzle from his glasses and continued. 'I broke and trained nearly all the horses for miles around,' he said.

'He really talks to 'em... you,' said Benjamin stopping abruptly as a rolled up blanket hit him on the side of the head followed by several more. The American prisoners scrabbled around excitedly to get their hands on one.

The prisoners opened them and wrapped them around their shoulders.

Everyone had a blanket except Dylan Chipp. 'Come on, can't one of you at least share a part with me?' he moaned.

Miles Longman was nearest to him and gave him a long hard penetrating stare with his huge dark eyes before slowly pulling the blanket tight across his shoulders and onto Dylan Chipp.

Dylan looked at him but gave no hint of thanks.

In the moonlight, the shadowy figures of Squire Irwin, Harold Thomson and two of his labourers stood anxiously and waited on an area of beach obscured by the overhanging cliffs. The Squire lit his pipe and pulled the match towards his pocket watch, flipped it open and squinted. 'It's about time, Mister Thomson,' he said.

'Yessir,' replied Harold Thomson.

He lit a lantern and waved it towards the sea trying desperately to obscure it from the land. A lantern flashed out at sea and a few minutes later a rowing boat glided towards the shore on the gentle waves.

The labourers pulled the craft onto the beach and with the help of Harold Thomson feverishly unloaded the crates, boxes and casks. Squire Irwin motioned to one of the labourers to open one of the casks. He tasted the contents, nodded, and handed over a small leather purse of sovereigns to the rower's accomplice.

While the crew dragged the boat back into the sea Harold and the labourers turned their attention to loading the horse drawn cart. Harold temporarily lost his grip on the largest cask but recovered before it hit the rocks and smashed.

'Be careful with that will yer,' cursed Squire Irwin in a stifled shout.

'Sorry, sir,' said Harold before tying the contraband onto the cart and moving off.

'Now get on with it... and keep the noise down or

you'll have every Revenue man in the county down on us,' he said as he kicked the sand from his boots before climbing onto his horse.

The labourers carefully guided the horse and cart up the beach and onto the coastal track.

After several hours they finally made their way between the groups of farm outbuildings and rode until they reached the farthest barn. They stopped at the entrance and one of the labourers took care to open the doors without making any sound, unhitched the horse, and dragged the cart inside.

They unloaded the cart in silence and stowed the crates and casks in a carefully prepared area beneath the straw. The Squire pulled a handful of coins from his waistcoat pocket and paid the labourers who disappeared into what was left of the night.

Squire Irwin tilted a cask and poured it into two wooden cups. 'Your good health, Mister Thomson,' he said as he downed the cognac. 'Not a bad night's work eh?'

'Indeed, sir,' replied Harold.

They both smiled in agreement congratulating themselves in silence while Squire Irwin reached into his other pocket and paid Harold.

While Harold Thomson made his way along the lane to his waiting horse the Squire checked the contraband was totally covered before closing the doors and double locking them.

The summer sun began to burn through the mist and slowly reached the prisoners who lay in a mass of cold and wet tangled bodies. Some of the militiamen stood guard while others walked slowly around the yard in an attempt to keep warm.

Peter Beck sat propped against the prison wall waiting for the door of Captain Shortland's office to open. As soon as he saw the Captain accompanied by Sergeant Greaves he painfully made to get up but the nearest militiamen immediately levelled their rifles threateningly towards him.

'Sir, I believe you're looking for me?' said Peter in a weak voice.

Captain Shortland smiled at Sergeant Greaves. 'What did I tell you, Sergeant? They're cowards, every last man of 'em,' he said. 'That's why they're here.'

He laughed loudly.

'Take 'em all away... except him,' he said pointing

aggressively at Peter. 'Throw him in the *cachot*,' he growled. The guards reached out, grabbed Peter and manhandled him towards the solid granite punishment block.

Benjamin awoke and screamed his protests as he made to run towards the guards but was restrained by Charles Francis and Miles Longman. He continued to struggle and managed to break loose and ran screaming towards Captain Shortland.

'Peter... what are you doing? Don't give in to those bastards!' he screamed.

'Let him get on with it,' shouted Dylan Chipp nodding enthusiastically. 'He deserved that, now perhaps we'll get something to eat and somewhere to sleep,' he said.

Sergeant Greaves cracked his whip and it coiled painfully around Benjamin's ankle causing him to fall heavily into the mud. He unwound it and like a man possessed, turned and raced back towards Dylan Chipp, only this time to be restrained by Joshua and Miles.

'Cum der, boy, we'm got plenty of dime fer dat,' whispered Joshua Amos.

The guards dragged Peter Beck up to the metal clad

door, waited for another guard to unlock it before throwing him into the intense darkness and slamming the heavy door behind him.

Peter landed heavily on the icy cold granite floor and lay shivering and shocked.

The remaining prisoners-of-war were each issued with a blanket, horse rug, woollen jacket, two yellow shirts, a pair of trousers, a waistcoat, a pair of wooden shoes and a woollen cap.

Dylan Chipp stopped and held up a yellow shirt with the letters "TO TO" stamped on the back, and in the centre, a thick arrow pointing upwards. 'What the hell is this?' he asked.

Sergeant Greaves moved towards him. 'TOTO... is the Transport Office,' he said as he straightened his body and stood upright as if he was about to the salute. 'They run this depot and don't you forget it,' he said before spitting wildly at the feet of Dylan.

Dylan Chipp took heed and led them out of the yard through a narrow granite gateway towards Number Three Block.

He stopped at the foot of the steps and shook with foreboding as he looked up at the moss covered granite walls that loomed high above him casting a heavy shadow across his already shocked face. He jumped back to avoid a rush of steaming urine and excrement that spewed from the open channels high above him. 'Filthy bastards!' he screamed.

Taking care to avoid the continuing effluent he nervously climbed the wide granite steps and entered the block. Narrow beams of sunlight found their way through the small unglazed slits cutting through the thick mist of condensation. The inmates lay in row upon row of hammocks, four and five high, coughing and moaning: a place of total horror and despair.

'What the…?' yelled Dylan as he held his nose in a vain attempt to reduce the stench.

As his eyes became accustomed to the bad light he screwed up his face in absolute revulsion. He picked his way through the semi-darkness treading in the pools of freezing water which had run down the walls. He stepped unknowingly into a puddle and jumped with shock as the icy water soaked into his already wet shoes.

'Christ… it's disgusting,' he moaned despondently.

'What the hell do you want?' echoed a voice from the darkness.

'Leave us alone will ya?' echoed another voice.

A painfully thin man swung with ease out of his hammock and stood directly in front of Benjamin. The prisoner tucked his armless sleeve inside his jacket before speaking.

'Charles Blasden, pleased to meet you,' he said his unshaven face partially hiding his toothless mouth. He smiled and pointed at the empty sleeve. 'Don't look so bloody shocked, I've still got the other one.' He raised it towards Benjamin's nose and touched his nostril. 'I lost it at Queenston Heights in....' Deep in thought, he subconsciously scratched wildly at his matted hair and pulled out a creeper. He clicked it hard between his filthy nails and checked it was dead before a smile slowly appeared on his tormented face. '...October 1812, that's right, 1812,' he said proudly.

Dylan Chipp turned to stare at him in disbelief. 'What do you call this? They can't expect me to stay in here,' he said in a frenzied voice.

The response was loud jeers which quickly built to a crescendo filling the damp cold air.

Another prisoner swung from his hammock knocking Dylan onto the slimy granite floor.

'Everyone gets treated the same here,' he paused, 'whoever you are,' said Marshall Cunningham in a strained high pitched voice. He reached forward and held out his hand but when Dylan noticed the jagged grotesque scar across his throat he pulled back in disgust.

'Please yerself, man,' said Marshall scratching at his bare chest. 'You'd better get used to it,' he said in a high pitched voice.

He tried to count the number of new prisoners but couldn't see. 'How many of you's are there anyhow?' he asked.

Charles Francis taken aback by the strangled voice emanating from such a large man trembled as he attempted to count the new prisoners. 'Ffff...,' he tried to speak but his voice faltered and faded away.

Dylan Chipp got to his feet and spouted forth. 'Come on man, there's fourteen of them and me.'

'Fifteen eh?' said Marshall. He thought for a second and pointed into the darkness. 'You can sleep back there.'

'With them?' questioned Dylan.

While Marshall stared at him, Miles Longman, Moses Reading, Joshua Amos and the others pushed past him.

'Not you's,' shouted Marshall, pointing at the black

prisoners. 'You three... get across to Number Four Block with the other black bastards,' he shouted. They stared at him in silence before finally turning away.

'No... hold on a minute... they belong to me,' exclaimed Dylan.

Marshall scratched his crotch wildly.

'All right... if they're gonna stay in this block you look after 'em,' he said. 'But upstairs.'

'Don't you three get any ideas, you still belong to me!' screamed Dylan Chipp.

While they ambled off Jeremiah Hatch pitched into the conversation from his hammock. 'The rest of ya had better find yerself a place or you'll end up on the floor and believe me it's not somewhere's even a dog would wanna be,' he said with a twisted smile.

'Sleep?' screamed Dylan. 'In here? I want to see the Agent!!' he continued, his face deep red with anger.

The inmates of the block burst into a deafening roar of laughter.

'I'm sorry, ma Lord,' said a new voice behind Dylan.

He turned to face yet another stranger and froze.

'Henry Sterling at your service, ma Lord,' said the tortured scar faced prisoner. With one eye and a deep socket where his other eye once was. 'I'm soooo sorry, ma Lord,' he repeated. He laughed loudly as he pulled the filthy patch over the empty eye socket.

The new arrivals jostled for a place to hang their hammocks and it was several minutes before they were all able to tie them in and stow their meagre belongings in the holes and crevices that previous prisoners had taken many weeks or months to cut in the granite walls and timber beams.

As dusk approached, the prisoners sat and waited impatiently for their first meal since arriving at the depot. Benjamin Beck found a space next to Jeremiah Hatch. 'Did you get those blankets to us?' asked Benjamin.

'Yeah, it's almost a ritual. Shortland tries to wear 'em all down,' he said taking a long drag on his pipe. 'We have an arrangement with one of the more amenable turnkeys.' He sniggered. 'They ain't *all* bad,' he said.

Marshall Cunningham and Asha Adams carried in a large wooden bucket of steaming broth and an armful of bread.

Dylan Chipp pushed his way to the front filled his plate and took a sip. 'Oargh! This tastes like horse shit!' He spat it out in disgust. 'Do you expect me to eat this?'

he moaned.

'Get stuck in. I've bin eating it for nearly two years and it ain't dun me no 'arm,' said Jeremiah.

'Speak for yerself,' said Henry Sterling as he turned to Dylan. 'Ma Lord wants stewed chicken. Is that right, ma Lord?' he squawked.

Dylan forced a half smile in agreement and when he realised that Henry was poking fun at him he threw the wooden plate in his direction.

In the darkness a prisoner screamed out, coughed hard, then choked and died.

Made visible only by the flickering light of militiaman's lamp outside the *cachot* Peter Beck and his sole companion saw two plates pushed through the eight inch square wicket in the metal clad door. They rushed towards it, grabbed at the bowls and ate the inedible broth voraciously.

In Number Three Block, the prisoners lay in their hammocks in pitch darkness, the air filled with hopeless moaning and groaning. They knew they were not alone, the hapless noises never stopped.

The air thick with the smell of urine and excreta, and

the condensed moisture on the ceiling dripped down onto the top row of hammocks while the remainder ran down the walls and onto the freezing granite floor.

'Marshall, are you awake?' whispered Benjamin.

'Yeah, I don't get much peace in 'ere,' replied Marshall.

'How long do you think they'll keep my brother in that place?' asked Benjamin.

'The *cachot*?' asked Marshall reflecting.

'Um,' replied Benjamin.

'Probably ten days,' said Marshall.

'Ten days?'

A stunned Benjamin tried to sit up but, realising he could fall out of his hammock, he steadied himself.

'He might get out sooner but I doubt it after what he did to Shortland,' said Marshall. 'I wished I'd seen it,' he laughed loudly. 'He's lucky to still be alive.'

'He'll never get through that,' said Benjamin.

''Course he will,' shouted a voice from the darkness.

'After the third time, it gets real hard,' said Marshall. 'You don't see many walk out or get carried out alive after that.'

'Third time, how you can just dismiss it like that?' he

asked.

'When you've spent as long here as we have you can't help but be scornful... but believe me some do come out alive,' he said reassuringly.

'He's sure got some space in there. The first one was too small, what with the trouble the Frenchies caused. Cotgrave had 'em build that one in 1811,' said Jeremiah.

'Cotgrave?' asked Benjamin.

'He was Shortland's predecessor. He was one hell of a mean bastard,' he said.

'Can you shut up!' screamed a voice.

'God help us,' shouted another.

Judith and Jonas Sleep sat close to the roaring log fire. The Captain plugged at his long pipe and subconsciously stroked his Irish wolfhound stretched out at his feet.

'Jonas, can I ask...?' she moved nervously in her chair waiting for a response. Her husband raised his head, looked across at her and waited for the question.

'What did happen to Thomas Irwin?' she asked.

He took another plug of his pipe. 'The short answer is that the wretched man is a coward and I had him flogged,' he said.

'Flogged?' she repeated. 'Well, I'm sure he deserved

it,' she said.

'Yes he did, he killed the American Captain in cold blood. Can you believe that? To make matters worse they had already surrendered and he was unarmed.' He took another drag on his pipe. 'He's one useless character, that's for sure,' he mumbled.

Judith gave his reply some thought and turned her attention to the flames.

Jonas pushed himself back into his chair and blew smoke towards the fire, a man at peace.

80Q3

ഇരു Chapter six ഇരു

Captain and Judith Sleep entered the tiny Princetown church of St Michael's and sat on the right side of the narrow aisle next to Isaac Hartman, Rachel and a sleeping baby Emily.

Squire Irwin and his family were already sat in the front row on the opposite side and, upon seeing the Captain, the Squire gave him a prolonged glower of contempt, and fidgeted uncomfortably in the pew.

The clergyman smiled and pointed to the hymn numbers on a board.

'Could we please sing together hymn number 263,' he said.

The organist played and the congregation stood and began to sing, *For those in peril on the sea.*

The choice of hymn clearly incensed the Squire who

turned to stare defiantly at Captain Sleep.

At the end of the service, the Squire, now fuming with rage, made to leave the church. His wife, Dorien, tugged at his sleeve and with the help of Thomas and Priscilla made a futile attempt to prevent him from leaving.

Captain and Judith Sleep left the church followed by Isaac Hartman, Rachel and baby Emily. Thomas, Squire Irwin and his wife were already outside the church gates and as soon as the Squire saw Captain Sleep he rushed across to him.

'Call yourself a Christian?' screamed Squire Irwin, shaking his head violently. 'You're not even human!'

Isaac Hartman strode across to join them. 'If I were you, sir, I would retract that statement. Captain Sleep is a fine naval officer, one of Nelson's own and an upstanding member of this community.' He paused and stared hard at Thomas. 'Something, sir... you might find hard to understand,' he said glibly.

The remainder of the congregation stood in silence and looked on.

'I beg your pardon, sir,' retorted the Squire.

Thomas Irwin kicked nervously at the gravel path. 'Sir, I think we should leave now,' he whispered.

Isaac overheard him.

'Squire, if I am permitted to offer an opinion, I feel that that would be a very wise decision,' he paused, 'sir!' said Isaac Hartman curtly.

Squire Irwin screwed up his face, his eyes almost disappearing beneath his bushy eyebrows. 'That's as maybe.' He coughed before continuing and turned to face Captain Sleep head on. 'But what you did is inexcusable.' His face reddened with anger. 'And you will pay!' he said. He turned to his wife, son and daughter. 'Come Dorien, Thomas, Priscilla,' he said brusquely.

Isaac Hartman made a move towards the Squire but Captain Sleep pulled him back.

'But, sir,' said Isaac.

'Leave him, he's really not worth it,' said the Captain.

Benjamin Beck, Henry Sterling and Asha Adams paced up and down in the thick mud.

Benjamin, deep in thought, stopped abruptly. 'So how long have you been in here, Asha?' he asked.

Asha thought for a moment and looked across at Henry before speaking.

'Well, when we first got captured they left me and

Henry on a filthy hulk on the Hamoaze and then after a few weeks we wuz marched to this place.'

'Through thick snow' interrupted Henry. 'I reckon it must be near on two years.' He thinks, 'but it was bad back in them days.'

'Bad then? So what do you think it's like now?' asked Benjamin. 'This place ain't no better than hell itself,' he said.

'That's as maybe but at least we got off that stinking hulk and we can see the sky.' He looked up at the clear sky and grinned. 'When me and Henry arrived the Frenchies were about leavin'. A lot of 'em 'ad bin in this place for nearly five years,' he said.

'Five years?' exclaimed Benjamin.

'That's right,' said Asha. 'The last of 'em only left in January, and as they was leavin' one poor bastard only had a piece of blanket to hand in to the soddin' rebels. When they saw it they sent 'im back inside. You should 'ave seen the poor sod he took it bad, real bad.' He shook his head and looked across to Henry.

Henry continued. 'He cut his own throat.' He swallowed hard and pointed to a spot between the closed gates. 'Right there,' he said softly, clearly affected by the memory.

'What did you expect? That Agent's one sonofabitch,' said Asha.

Charles Blasden pushed himself forward. 'That's an understatement, Cotgrave was bad... but Shortland!' He paused. 'Bloody Shortland, he's a real hard bastard.'

'How come there was still a French prisoner out on the moor the day we arrived?' asked Benjamin.

'A few of the sickest ones, not fit to travel stayed on in the infirmary 'til they was well enough to leave,' said Asha.

'And Shortland had his eye on that one for quite a while. We knew he'd never see France again,' said Charles staring blankly into space.

Peter Beck sat on the floor of the *cachot* and shivered, cold and hungry and feeling extremely dejected. As the outside lantern blew in the wind casting a flash of light into the cell his cellmate moved close to him and he saw him for the first time.

'You're a *mulatto*, how come you're in here?' asked a surprised Peter.

'Me mudder wuz Negro slave und I's reckon me fadda wuz de plandation munager... dey musd 'ave gut togedda ya know... somehow's.' He laughed and stood up. 'Dat man... 'e 'ave a but ov a reputation fer dat. I dink 'e earn da money frum de owner fer effery mixed race babie 'e faddered,' he said.

He kicked at the granite wall and sat down. 'Et didn't 'elp... I's still a slave, prob'ly 'ways will be zo.'

'Um...,' muttered Peter, not knowing what to say.

'I wuz in Numba Fer Block wi' de rest of the sleves and Dick tuk a big 'atin' to me, said I wuz a white sonofabitch... I 'ad to defend maself... I's stubbed one of dem... killed em....'

Peter interrupted him. 'From what I've seen over the past few weeks I wouldn't have thought the British would have cared one way or another about that.'

'You's right... but den I stubbed a Sergeant.'

Peter smiled and nodded. 'Kill him?' he asked eagerly.

The mulatto shook his head. 'No, zir... I wounded 'im... Sergeant Greaves... no need ta see MacGrath... nottin' more dan a scratch,' he said the dejection clear in his voice.

''Nuff of dat,' he said as he reached out his hand. 'Me naeme is Uriah... Uriah Spearman.'

Peter smiled. 'Pleased to meet you, Uriah Spearman,' he said. 'Peter Beck, I'm in here with my younger brother Benjamin.'

'Fast dime I'd 'eard a dat.... Cousans... course, but bruvvers... um.'

'I didn't want to join the navy, Benjamin convinced me to go with him... biggest mistake we could have made...,' said Peter shaking his head. 'Don't know if or when we'll ever get outta here,' he said reflecting.

'Look... don't ya give up, mon,' said Uriah. 'Come on... dis war'll be over zoon und we go 'ome... e'en me... a slave,' he said as he contemplated his future.

During the night the door opened and Uriah was removed.

Peter never saw him again. And nor did anyone else.

Ten days later the *cachot* door opened again and Peter Beck looking frail and exhausted, leaned against the frame, put on his glasses, tilted his head backwards and cried to himself as the sudden freezing rain beat down onto his pale face.

Benjamin ran across to help his elder brother but Sergeant Greaves held him back, threatening him with his bullwhip.

'If I was you, I'd try to keep out of the way of the Captain.' He said to Peter as he fingered his whip lovingly. 'Or next time... he'll see yer dead.' He laughed in Peter's face and walked away.

Benjamin supported his brother and motioned to Henry Sterling to help him. Reluctantly he edged his way across the yard to join them.

'Come on Peter, I've saved you something to eat,' said Benjamin turning to stare back at Sergeant Greaves. 'Bastard,' he mouthed.

As they made their way to Number Three Block, dark leaden clouds rolled in across the depot and the thick mist descended over them.

The torrential rain hammered on the roof of the building and, while two prisoners washed and brushed the granite floor, Dylan Chipp lay in his hammock shivering and mumbling to himself. He finally slid out and prodded his neighbour's hammock.

'Come on, get up!' he shouted.

The prisoner rolled out of his hammock and fell to the ground with a deathly thud.

Dylan ran towards the door screaming while the two prisoners, unaffected by the dead body, continued to sweep around it.

Benjamin wrapped his brother in a blanket and passed him the food he had saved for him.

'How do you feel now?' asked Benjamin.

The noise and shouting at the far end of the building almost drowned him out.

'I'll be all right, but the poor sod I met in there didn't make it,' said Peter Beck sadly screwing up his face. 'He'd bin in there for weeks... then they took...,' he murmured.

'Get some sleep,' said Benjamin thinking. 'If you can.'

At the far end of the block Dylan Chipp collected money from the other prisoners.

'Any more bets?' he shouted, the excitement clearly audible in his grating voice.

William Cole held up a sixpenny piece. Dylan grabbed it, nodded his acceptance and slipped it unnoticed into his waistcoat pocket.

'That's it, Robert. It's closed,' he said assertively.

The prisoners moved back, formed a large circle against the walls and stood in silence. Robert Stapely signalled to young Sylas and he pulled out a large stinking bone from a hessian sack and dropped it in the middle of the circle.

They stood motionless and waited patiently.

A large rat pushed its nose out of a hole and scurried across to the bone. Other rats followed and within seconds there were nearly a dozen rats gnawing at the rotting bone.

Ralph Etherington, the appointed adjudicator, whistled loudly and the rats scurried back to their holes. The prisoners screamed, cheered and whistled loudly.

Ram Barley jumped in the air. 'I won... I won!' he screamed with excitement.

Ralph Etherington stepped forward. 'You didn't,' he said.

'I tell you, I did,' said an indignant Ram Barley.

'I tell ya now.' Ralph looked around for any agreement. There wasn't any. He swallowed before he continued. 'You didn't,' repeated Ralph.

'William won!' said a confident Dylan Chipp.

As William Cole reached for his winnings Ram Barley pulled a knife from his boot and lashed out at him slicing deep into his arm.

'That's enough,' shouted Ralph. 'William won fair and square,' he said as he forced himself between the gamblers.

Ram Barley pulled his knife away and wiped it on his sleeve before he stormed off in a rage, cursing under his breath.

ಬಿ൩ಬ

ഇൟ **Chapter seven** ഇൟ

The heavily laden pony train weaved its way across the moor, led by Martha, an overweight middle aged trader. She sat uncomfortably on the leading pony followed by Helmut Fischer, a German Jew, Freda, the bearded fish wife, who wore fishermen's boots and jacket and other traders and moorland farmers who joined the procession as it neared the prison.

Upon reaching the Dartmoor depot the outer gates swung opened and the traders were permitted to pass slowly through the narrow opening. They were searched by the militia and guards who weighed their goods and chalked up the weight and price on each sack or basket before allowing them to pass through the second gate.

Agnes, a pretty young girl, struggled with two baskets as she made her way towards the gate. After the guard checked the contents of her baskets she was permitted to join the rest of the traders in the inner courtyard. The courtyard also served as the market square where the traders and locals were permitted to sell their produce between the hours of eleven in the morning until two o'clock in the afternoon, throughout the week except Sunday.

The early morning sun shone across the square highlighting the contrasting and colourful traders at their respective stalls.

Martha has two stalls of vegetables, peat and bread, behind which her ponies struggled to get at the few strands of hay she had left for them.

The prisoners crowded excitedly around Agnes's stall and fought to ogle her while others queued to buy her saffron cakes. In contrast, Freda stood desperately trying to sell her rotting merchandise to a few emaciated Negroes who hung belligerently around her fish stall.

While other stalls sold homemade bread and cakes, meat, straw and leather, Helmut Fischer straightened up his rolls of cloth, buttons and calico while another Jewish trader alongside him set out his stall of tobacco.

The depot square was packed. Prisoners, militia,

guards and members of the public pushed their way through the crowd and walked from stall to stall before deciding where they would spend their money.

A very large crowd of local people haggled enthusiastically around a stall near the Barter Gate, where Ralph Etherington was selling delicate objects, small forks, spoons, canon, carts and small ships, intricately carved by his fellow prisoners from stolen beef and mutton bones which, now highly polished, could pass for ivory.

Thomas Irwin studied a tiny figurine but as he turned he accidentally bumped into a pretty young woman and dropped it onto the ground.

'You'll 'ave to pay for that if it's damaged, sir,' shouted Ralph angrily.

'What the...?' cursed Thomas Irwin as he bent down and groaned with pain as he picked up the figurine.

'I'm very sorry, sir,' said the young woman, her long dark hair glistening in the sun.

Still holding his back, Thomas turned. 'Hello Mara... how are you?' he asked.

'Hello Thomas, I'm fine thank you.'

She took her time to look him up and down. 'Are you

feeling any better?' she asked.

Thomas looked at her surprised. 'You heard?' he said.

'Father told me,' she said nodding gracefully.

'Ah...' he paused nervously. 'I... I... I... saved First Lieutenant Hartman's life by shooting that Yankee Captain,' he said forcing a smile. 'And what does Captain Sleep do?' He paused and waited but she didn't reply. 'He had me flogged, that's what... the bas... had me flogged,' he seethed, not attempting to hide the contempt in his voice.

Mara feigned an impressed smile. 'So you're a hero?' she said.

William Cole shared a joke with Joshua Amos and accidentally bumped into Mara.

'I'm sorry, ma'am,' he said graciously.

'No... it was my fault,' she said looking around. 'It's awfully crowded this morning,' she said before turning to Thomas. She gave him an obviously false smile. 'It's good to see you again, Thomas,' she said before returning to William.

'Likewise, Mara,' said Thomas, scowling at William Cole before walking off.

'I'm very sorry, ma'am but if I may say so I wouldn't

become too friendly with... that character,' he said loud enough for Thomas to hear.

She smiled, lowered her head, and walked off deep in thought.

The Rough Alleys, a group of filthy anti-social thieves who had absolutely no scruples and revelled in crime and violence, came together because of their common depravity. They gathered in the corner of the market and openly planned their next crime. Without a word of warning the group attacked Helmut, the Jewish stall holder, wrecking his stall before being chased away by a group of bayonet thrusting militiamen who, although appearing brave on the surface, were very wary at having to challenge the most vicious of inmates.

In the chaos Marshall Cunningham seized the opportunity and delicately fingered a length of cloth on Helmut Fischer's stall. With the other hand, unnoticed, he attached a hook to a second piece of material. He dropped the cloth silently to the ground, looked furtively around, and nodded. Robert Stapely pulled at the cord and it began to slide along the floor under the stall and out of site into a nearby grating.

Later that afternoon, while the rain hammered onto

the roof of Number Three Block and the prisoners-of-war sat talking and singing, Dylan Chipp was being measured for a new suit by the best tailor in the depot, a Negro from Number Four Block, courtesy of Big Dick.

'Look at that bastard. As soon as he gets money, what does he do? Waste it on a new suit!' shouted William Cole.

'He's gonna look like Royalty,' screamed Marshall Cunningham before turning to face Dylan Chipp. 'Is that right, ma Lord?' he chortled.

'Who's gonna see it in 'ere?' shouted Asha Adams.

'You might all laugh but we're gonna be out of here by Christmas,' retorted Dylan as he stroked the stolen cloth.

Jeremiah Hatch sat playing dice with Ram Barley. 'Is that right the British took Washington?' he asked.

'Yeah! They sure did,' replied Ram Barley. 'They took the White House back in August, President Madison and the rest of Congress had to high tail it outta there.'

'They did what?' asked a surprised Marshall Cunningham.

'They had to. The bastards darn well burnt the White House to the ground,' he said. 'But as I took off for sea again, I heard we beat 'em at Baltimore and the British high tailed it back to Canada,' he said before throwing a double six.

Marshall Cunningham made his way across to Peter Beck. 'How ya doin'?' he asked.

'I'm fine now. Just glad to be out of that hole,' he said as he fingered his glasses case. 'What happened to you?' he asked pointing at Marshall's jagged scar across his throat.

'A group of Rough Alleys attacked me when I got me allowance,' he said as he recalled the moment. 'If I were you I'd keep out of their way, they'll kill anybody for a penny,' he said.

'The evil bas...,' cursed Peter, as Marshall Cunningham cut off Peter in full flow. 'It's all right, I was lucky. William Dykar, Doc MacGrath's predecessor, wanted to cut me head off to save me life,' he said laughing loudly. 'The old bastard saved me life all right. I don't think I'd be 'ere now if MacGrath had got to me,' he said in his high pitched voice.

Tavistock was alive with the annual October Goosey Fayre. Martha, Agnes, Helmut and all the prison traders had set up their stalls in the narrow streets which were crammed with farm animals, stalls selling everything imaginable, traders, buskers, fire eaters, and pen upon pen of white geese.

In the centre of the square a Punch and Judy booth had already attracted a large crowd of children and adults. A puppet dressed like a French soldier dodged the wooden baton waved aggressively at him by Mister Punch who screamed uncontrollably at him in a blood curdling high pitched voice.

Isaac and Rachel Hartman, Captain and Judith Sleep stood at the rear of the crowd and joined in the fun. Isaac moved close to Captain Sleep and waiting for a break in the jeering, whispered in his ear. 'Captain, would you and Judith do us the honour of being Godparents to our Emily?'

The Captain nodded slowly, turned and smiled. 'We'd be highly honoured... highly honoured,' he said proudly.

The crowd's raucous laughter drowned out any further conversation.

"Soooo... the Frenchies tried to beat us!' shrieked Mister Punch.

'Yeah!' shouted the crowd hanging on his every

word.

'And what did Wellington do?' replied Mister Punch.

The crowd now at fever pitch built to a crescendo.

'Chased Napoleon all the way to Elba,' they yelled.

Mister Punch tossed the French puppet into the air with his baton and caught him again.

As the crowd went wild Monsieur Boulan, a well dressed, French, ex-prisoner shrugged in disgust and disappeared unnoticed into the crowd.

Mister Punch then dragged a puppet dressed in a jacket fashioned in a miniature Star Spangled Banner flag, erected a hangman's gallows and stood holding the noose in his hand.

'And what are we going to do with them Yankees?' shrieked Mister Punch.

'Hang 'em,' screamed the crowd.

'Hang 'em all,' yelled a disabled seaman at the back.

'Lock 'em up and throw away the key,' shouted a voice deep in the crowd.

The crowd jeered loudly in agreement.

Mister Punch pushed the American puppet into the noose and hit him viciously with his baton. 'That's the way to do it!' he screamed and the crowd agreed wholeheartedly with their jeers and shouts.

Dylan Chipp stood in the prison yard and talked animatedly to a group of Rough Alleys and within an hour they carried two old dented boilers into Number Three Block. They delivered them to an excited Dylan Chipp who was standing in the shadows in the furthest corner of the block.

'Over here... over here,' he repeated in a strained whisper finding it hard to hide his excitement.

The Rough Alleys carried them to him. Dylan paid them, covered them with an old sack and stood smirking and congratulating himself. 'No one beats Dylan Chipp,' he repeated over and over.

The next morning Dylan Chipp waited impatiently outside the back door of the kitchen. It slowly opened and a porter passed him a tightly rolled up cloth. Dylan grabbed at it, paid him, and rushed off towards the market square.

While Robert Stapley filled a large can with water from the open channel that ran through the prison yard Dylan Chipp opened the cloth, checked the burnt bread crusts and burnt peas, rewrapped them and beat them hard against the wall.

Hatred is the key

Robert struggled across the yard with the heavy can of water and poured it into the metal boilers while Dylan shook with anticipation. 'Come on get it in there boy,' he said as he lit the fire beneath the boilers and waited. As soon as the water boiled he carefully sprinkled the fine crumbs and smashed peas into the bubbling water, stood back and waited. His impatience was clear as he sub consciously alternated between tapping his feet and digging his heels hard into the gravel.

As the long forgotten intoxicating aroma wafted across the square the prisoners began to gather around him. Dylan stood back and mumbled to himself. 'I'll show 'em who's smart.'

The corner of the market square was ready to burst as the excited prisoners crowded around Dylan Chipp and Robert Stapley. They both stood proudly beside the steaming coffee and tea boilers. The prisoners, each holding their own mugs, had already formed a queue which reached for several yards, as they waited to buy their hot drinks.

'This is how it should be boy,' he said firmly. 'You keep an eye on 'em, and remember... no money... no tea or coffee,' he said with a controlling voice and a wide smile. He walked along the line collecting the pennies while Robert carefully poured equal measures of coffee and tea. When the coffee ran out he removed some of the liquid from the boiler containing the tea, poured it into the coffee boiler and topped it up.

മാരു

౸ೞ Chapter eight ౸ೞ

The thick dark clouds rushed across the sky passing low across the Tor.

The wild northerly wind blew the long gone summer's dead heather and gorse across the muddy farm yard, attacking the branches of the ancient oaks that surrounded the farmstead and violently stripping the remaining leaves from them.

Henrietta and Alex chased the sheep into their pen and closed the gate behind them before running towards the cottage clearly uneasy as the loose and rotten timbers rattled noisily on the outbuildings around them.

'Winter's gonna be 'ere early this year. You mark me words,' shouted their father, Harold Thomson, his voice barely audible above the wind.

A few minutes later the first snow of the winter began

to fall across the moor.

Dylan Chipp lay, in his hammock in the darkness and after carefully counting his money, smiled and congratulated himself. He scratched at his chest, picked off a creeper, looked at it closely and grunted in disgust before squeezing it between his filthy finger nails.

The next morning the prison yard was dusted with a thin layer of snow.

Some of the prisoners exercised in the snow covered yard and played football to keep warm while other sickly, prisoners leant against the wall, coughing and shivering and trying desperately to catch what was left of the weak sun on their pale and gaunt faces.

The ball was kicked over the wall, a guard kicked it back and the game continued.

The last rays of the mid December sun shone into the Agent's office illuminating the collection of oil paintings of ships and various maps and charts of the New World, while along another wall stood a rack of rifles loaded and ready for use.

The air was heavy with the smoke.

Rueben G Beasly, the overweight American with the

twin titles of American Agent and American Consul, sat at one side of the large solid oak desk, smoking a huge cigar, while Captain Shortland paced up and down taking huge drags on his cigar.

'It's not good enough, Mister Beasly,' he said. 'Don't you realise?' He swallowed angrily, 'that you as the American representative, are neglecting your own citizens.'

The American tried to catch his breath. 'Captain, you don't need me to tell you how long it takes for instructions to arrive from my country.' He had to think before he continued. 'The last took... almost seven weeks.' He took another deep breath. 'And, if you were to ask me how long the next communication will take... well... I've absolutely no idea.' He forced a smile and slumped back in his chair. 'Britain has control of the seas.' He shook his head in desperation. 'I'm doing all I can,' he said as he stroked his double chin and massaged it while shaking his head from side to side.

'Come, come, Mister Beasly,' said Captain Shortland who stood looking out onto the yard. 'That's as maybe but you have the power to release more of their rightful allowance.' He turned to face Beasly. 'Who knows how much longer,' he coughed loudly, 'our guests will be here?'

'Very well, Captain... when I return to London I will make arrangements to release two months allowance to our fellow citizens of one penny halfpenny a day for distribution by your goodself.' He sat forward and took a huge drag on his cigar before continuing. 'But there is little else I am permitted to do,' he said exhaling a cloud of smoke.

Isaac Hartman struggled with a fir tree cut from the nearby forest and forced his way through the snow fighting the strong biting wind every inch of the way.

Rachel tidied the sitting room while the wind whistled eerily around the longhouse.

In stark contrast to the weather outside, the small and compact room was welcoming and warmed by the log fire that roared in the open stone fireplace.

The flames created dancing shadows across the white lime washed ceiling and walls.

Isaac stumbled exhausted into the cottage, kicked the snow from his sodden boots and placed them close to the fire. Rachel took his overcoat and placed it on a wooden hanger and hung it on the extended granite mantelshelf away from the fire, rubbed the remaining ice from his boots before she straightened and turned them sole up and placed them away on the end of the hearth away from the fierce flames.

This was the first time Isaac had been home for Christmas since marrying Rachel a few years earlier and with his new family decided to follow in his Captain's footsteps by having a tree.

Captain Sleep had been one of the first people on Dartmoor to erect a Christmas tree. He learnt of the tradition when he visited Hamburg in the winter of 1805, a few short months before the arrival of Napoleon's troops who were to occupy the strategically placed city and port for many years.

Isaac reached into his waistcoat pocket and took out his razor sharp knife and trimmed the branches of the perfect tree that would soon fill one corner of the room. He placed the redundant branches on the fire, causing it to smoke heavily before bursting into life and creating high flames which temporarily filled the room with a brilliant bright light.

Isaac moved the tree from one place to the next before finally positioning it and standing back proudly to admire it.

'It's beautiful, absolutely beautiful, darling,' said Rachel excitedly. 'Look at it Emily, isn't it wonderful?'

Emily slept unaware of the transformation going on around her.

While Isaac had been away at sea, Rachel had spent many long hours making decorative needle and bobbin lace in the form of snowflakes and contemporary Italian tassles which she carefully adapted to resemble icicles. She had been fortunate enough to have met a Honiton lace maker in Tavistock market who taught her the intricate process.

Together the couple carefully chose where to hang the lace decorations, apples and chestnuts, sprigs of holly, dried flowers and shaped coloured paper.

Rachel leaned across and lovingly kissed Isaac's cheek. 'It's good to have you here with us,' she purred.

Isaac smiled at her lovingly, 'I'm going to be around for a while longer.' He grinned at her. 'The Captain visited Plymouth yesterday...,' his grin gradually turned into a huge smile. 'The *Raytheon* won't be ready until at least the end of April.'

Rachel moved closer to her husband, cuddled and

kissed him gently, while subconsciously her forefinger followed the line of his carefully sculpted sideburns.

'They can take as long as they wish… it's so good to have you here with us.' She looked across lovingly at Emily in the handmade crib. 'Isn't it Emily?'

She kissed Isaac again. 'Perhaps she'll be walking before you leave us?'

Isaac smiled. 'I should hope so,' he said looking down at Emily.

The prison kitchens were noisier than normal as the cooks prepared what in their opinion was a special Christmas meal. It was no different than any other day but to them they knew they would have a short respite from their usual mundane duties. Due to the poor weather only limited ingredients had arrived from the outside victuallers and therefore the food was prepared quicker than normal.

With everything prepared the last porter blew out the oil lamps as he left and walked out of the door closing it behind him. In the darkness, dozens of large well-fed rats crawled out from behind boxes, crates, sacks and rubbish bins and made their way to the uncovered cauldrons of cooling broth.

In the clear frosty afternoon the liveried carriage of Sir Thomas Tyrwhitt, followed by a number of other carriages, made their way up the long gravel drive towards the imposing country residence of Squire Irwin.

Stuffed animal heads adorned every wall of the large oak panelled entrance hall while a large Christmas tree took pride of place at the foot of the wide sweeping staircase.

The Squire and his family welcomed their guests with a large glass of hot punch.

'Happy Christmas, Sir Thomas,' beamed Squire Irwin holding his glass high in the air.

In stark contrast a solitary branch of holly hung from the beam in Number Three Block and many of the prisoners sat along the wall and read the first letters since arriving at the Depot. It was biting cold and others lay in their hammocks shivering, coughing and moaning. Other groups of prisoners smoked, played cards and games while Peter Beck tried to pick out a tune on a mandolin he had won in a game of cards.

'The British are givin' us a hell of a fight up in Canada,' said Ram Barley as he read his letter aloud.

'We're gonna win though ain't we?' asked Sylas nervously.

''Course we are son..., give it time,' reassured Peter Beck stopping briefly before picking at the strings once more.

Robert Stapely broke down. 'Are we ever gonna get out of 'ere? I just wanna go home,' he cried.

His outburst visibly affected them all.

'Who would have thought that we would be spending Thanksgiving and now Christmas like this?' said Ram Barley.

Dylan Chipp resplendent in his new suit walked into the centre of the group and stood preening himself in front of an imaginary mirror.

'I can't believe I'm spending Christmas in prison,' he paused and slowly looked around. 'With slaves and gamblers,' he said with a sly grin.

Ram Barley slowly got to his feet. 'How can you say that? The wanton gambling paid for that suit of yours.' He took a moment to think before continuing. 'And as for the slaves, well....' He raised his voice, 'they haven't done you any harm,' he shouted.

Ralph Etherington and Marshall Cunningham carried

the food into the block lit by the few oil lamps which hung from the wall by makeshift hooks of pieces of bone and rusty nails.

Everyone sat on the floor waiting their turn but true to form Dylan Chipp rushed to the front and pushed his plate towards Ralph Etherington for the first serving.

Ralph dipped the ladle deep into the metal bowl and poured it onto Dylan Chipp's plate.

'Look at this!' screamed Dylan as he pushed his fingers nervously into the steaming broth and pulled at the black tail to reveal a whole boiled rat. 'They're feeding us rats!' he screamed as he threw the bowl at Ralph.

'Wot da ya expect, mon? Dis es Christmus,' screeched Miles laughing loudly.

Moses sniggered. 'Why am you zo dif'rent frum uz? Haf ya ever dought wut ya gif uz ta eat bak 'ome?' he said.

'You boy! Are a slave,' said Charles Francis with a look of total disgust. 'Ugh, why should we waste decent food on the likes of you?' he screeched.

Dylan Chipp finally laughed.

Moses shook his head and began to get to his feet.

'You bastard!' he shouted.

'What did you say?' shouted Charles Francis as he pulled a knife from his boot, lunged at Moses and cut deep into the main artery of his arm.

Blood began to pump uncontrollably out of the black slave's veins.

'I told ya... you ain't like us, boy... you never will be,' screamed an incensed Charles Francis.

Miles reached forward and grabbed at his throat. He threw his head back and forward and after a bitter fight choked the life out of Charles Francis before turning his attention to Dylan Chipp.

'Get away from me, boy! I'll have you hung for that,' screamed Dylan looking around for someone, anyone to agree with him.

Undeterred, Miles punched him hard in the stomach and around the head, cutting his mouth and breaking his nose before being pulled off.

Charles Blasden stepped forward and grabbed at Dylan with his only arm. 'We make our own justice in 'ere,' he screamed. He looked down and pointed firmly at the body of Charles Francis. 'And that's justice,' he said as he spat at the body.

Miles turned his attention to Moses and after ripping a thin strip from his shirt sleeve tied it around his heavily bleeding arm.

The trouble was suddenly brought to a halt as the turnkey blew his horn. 'Turn in! Turn in!' he shouted as he slammed the inner door with a loud echoed bang and locked it. With the first door locked behind him he walked to the outer door and slammed it shut. Leaving everyone to reflect on what had just happened.

In a distinct contrast to Number Three Block huge logs burned in the large carved granite fireplace beneath a portrait of Squire Irwin resplendent in his finest heavily embroidered clothes. The oak panelled walls, beautiful plaster cornices, the heavy velvet drapes, were a backdrop for the laid up mahogany dining table with the silver cutlery, ornate crystal cut glasses, matching decanters and beautiful silver candlesticks.

The atmosphere was noisy and jovial.

The Squire and his wife Dorien, Thomas and Priscilla Irwin, Captain Shortland and Mara, Sir Thomas Tyrwhitt and Doctor George MacGrath sat around the table. All the gentlemen had already consumed a great deal of alcohol and although dinner was almost finished in the centre of the gigantic table huge plates and dishes that appeared to have hardly been touched still overflowed with a immense piece of ribbed beef, a leg of ham, a partially eaten goose, roasted potatoes, whole parsnips and other assorted root vegetables.

'A wonderful table of food Squire Irwin... complements to the kitchen,' said Doctor MacGrath.

They all clapped appreciatively.

Sir Thomas waited for the clapping to subside before speaking. 'The Prince Regent tells me Napoleon is trying to put a new army together,' he said hardly able to contain himself. 'To fight again,' he laughed loudly, 'that's right... to fight again!' he bellowed.

'Surely he's already learnt his lesson? He knows he won't be welcome in France and if he knows what's good for him he'll stay in Elba,' said Captain Shortland.

The Squire gave the butler a nod and he left the room unnoticed.

'We'll just have to wait and see... but gentlemen don't underestimate him, he is a very determined man,' said Sir Thomas.

'Or, totally mad!' shouted Captain Shortland emptying his glass in one gulp.

The butler returned to the room holding two bottles of Cognac and stood unnoticed in the corner awaiting further instructions.

'I'm sure Wellington won't mind beating him for the second time, eh?' said Captain Shortland.

Squire Irwin coughed and grinned widely. 'Enough of that, Gentlemen,' he paused and waited for their full attention. 'Now, would you care to try something, dare I say a little different and very, very special?' he said.

They signalled their agreement and the butler proceeded to walk around the table pouring everyone a glass.

'Your good health, gentlemen,' said Squire Irwin as he raised his glass.

They swirled the blonde liquid around before they finally sipped it and smiled broadly in agreement before taking a much larger drink.

'A very fine Cognac, Robert,' said Captain Shortland as he emptied his glass. 'Very fine,' he repeated with a wide drunken smile of deep satisfaction. Without warning, he reached towards the butler and grabbed one of the bottles before anyone realised what was happening. He poured himself a large measure and emptied the glass before letting out a loud a raucous laugh. 'Very fine indeed,' he slurred.

'It should be, it's made by an Englishman in Jarnac, a Thomas Hine, and certainly very special... and... may I say extremely expensive.' He laughed loudly and winked. 'I'll arrange a bottle for you, Captain. And of course for yourself, Sir Thomas,' said Squire Irwin.

'Sir, that would be much appreciated,' said Sir Thomas. 'Now, I would like to propose a toast to our host and hostess,' he said raising his glass.

They all raised their glasses.

'Merry Christmas,' they said collectively.

The Squire finally put down his glass and looked thoughtfully across to Sir Thomas. 'Is it right that the highwayman, Tom Rocket has been hanged?' he asked.

Sir Thomas took a slug of his Cognac. 'Yes, it is....' He answered and reflected. 'Um... a great pity.'

'What?' boomed Captain Shortland. 'He was a robber, a highwayman no less, robbing those poor and unfortunate souls between Honiton and Exeter.'

'That's as maybe, Captain but he was most courteous to the end. The hangman over in Exeter was very upset at having to administer the punishment... most upset...

most upset indeed.'

'I hear tell he was a former army captain,' asked Squire Irwin.

Sir Thomas nodded. 'That's correct... a tall and powerfully built young man of thirty five years.' He reflected. 'So be it... Justice has to reign or we'd have anarchy.' He turned to Captain Shortland. 'Is that right, Captain?'

Captain Shortland nodded and lit another cigar.

While the rest of the inmates sat on the floor playing cards, rereading their letters or singing, a bloodied and pained Dylan Chipp sat well away from everyone else and sub consciously fingered the soft fabric of his left jacket sleeve. In the poor light he ran his hands down the other sleeve of his jacket until he felt a creeper and revolted at its very presence jumped up cursing to himself. He spent the next hour carefully examining every inch of his suit meticulously removing any obvious dirt and searching for any other invasive bugs.

Moses Reading lay in the corner slowly bleeding to death. Miles knelt over him. 'Prumis me, ya woon't let 'im take me back,' moaned Moses as he turned his head in the direction of Dylan Chipp. 'I'd radda die dan ge back ta dat,' he gasped.

'We woon't,' replied Miles with tears in his eyes. 'We'm go up t' north togedda,' he lied.

Moses struggled to speak. 'Prumis me,' he said in a whisper before his whole body shuddered and he died.

'I prumis,' mouthed Miles.

He reached down and closed his dead friend's eyes and covered him with a blanket before getting up and walking slowly towards Dylan Chipp.

'I's gunna kill ya,' he slurred at Dylan.

Dylan muttered his disagreement.

'What did you say? You bastard?' asked Dylan Chipp.

Henry leaned across and whispered to Dylan. 'Say nothing, we'll get our chance,' he said reassuringly.

Peter Beck jumped up throwing his mandolin to the ground. 'That's enough!' he screamed, his voice reverberating off the granite walls. 'Are we all gonna kill each other?'

He looked around for some agreement.

There was none.

He remembered what Uriah told him in the *cachot*. 'That's exactly what they want us to do.' He paused and shook his head in dismay before walking off into the darkness.

The next morning the snow covered yard was crammed with prisoners as the bodies of Moses Reading and Charles Francis were carried in silence towards the infirmary.

William Cole broke the silence. 'We're all gonna die in here. If we don't end up killing each other, or disease get us,' he shouted, 'this place will!'

He stomped off across the yard in silence as his fellow prisoners slowly realised that what he had just said was probably true.

ഇരുൽ

❧ **Chapter nine** ❧

Following the decision by the Transport Office to concentrate most of the American prisoners-of-war in Dartmoor depot a new party of prisoners from Chatham arrived as the heavy mist descended once more upon the prison. Some were obviously injured and lay moaning in carts while others stood shivering, wet and cold outside the gates in the hard packed snow.

The gates opened and the fit prisoners were marched through while the sick and injured were lifted off the carts and carried in on makeshift stretchers to the infirmary.

A very drunk Captain Shortland walked out of his office slouched against the door frame and slowly eyed the prisoners one at a time. 'No one escapes from here,' he slurred. 'And I mean no one.' He belched loudly took a swig at his whiskey and turned. 'Sergeant, take them away!' he shouted. 'Put them in Number Four Block with the black bastards and Big Dick,' he raged.

Number Four Block was ruled by Big Dick, a Negro who was given his nickname because he stood some six foot four inches tall and towered above most if not all his fellow prisoners. This block had become notorious since the Americans arrived and was soon overflowing with black prisoners and any misfits that were unfortunate to be incarcerated in the depot. An unwritten agreement between Captain Cotgrave, Shortland's predecessor, and the fierce Negro permitted him to rule the block with a rod of iron providing he kept them under control and out of trouble with other prisoners. Dick maintained order with regular floggings for anyone who failed to obey his orders. He was often seen wearing a bearskin cap and carrying a heavy club as he regularly inspected his *"domain"* meting out floggings to anyone who failed to follow his orders.

Sergeant Greaves cracked his whip, licked his lips and smiled. 'Let's have yer,' he shouted. 'Get a move on,' he said.

The prisoners started to move but had no idea in which direction they should go and tripped over each other some slipping on the frozen mud and snow. Sergeant Greaves immediately cracked his whip three times at the prisoners in quick succession; their faces unable to hide the sheer terror.

Doctor George MacGrath walked slowly through the packed infirmary of the sick and dying prisoners checking them as he walked. The orderlies carried in the latest sick arrivals and the Doctor stopped to address them. 'How many this time?' he sighed, his voice tired and faint.

The orderly looked to the stretchers behind him. 'Six,' he replied.

The second orderly following him spoke out. 'And there's nearly a dozen more from block three on their way.'

'Typhus and smallpox is wiping them out quicker than last year's measles epidemic or the African pox,' he said as he looked around in desperation. 'Put 'em over there,' said Doctor MacGrath, his voice almost inaudible amongst the coughs and moans as he pointed to the empty spaces. The orderlies followed his instruction and laid the new patients on the cold granite floor between the more fortunate sick prisoners who lay on thin straw mattresses infested with creepers and fleas.

As the snow began to fall heavily, the sentinels moved into their makeshift shelters and watched over the freezing prisoners as they exercised in the yard to keep warm. But as dusk approached and visibility diminished the sentries were called down from the walls and returned to the warmth of the guard house.

In Number Three Block, a lone oil lamp hanging from the timber beam shed deep and heavy shadows across the ceiling. The prisoners lay in their hammocks in semi darkness, coughing, sneezing and moaning. The breath condensed on the walls and formed sheets of ice while the residue fell onto the granite floor and immediately froze. A bedeviled prisoner ran screaming between the occupied hammocks, hammered at the door and slumped to the ground.

'Robert just died,' shouted a voice in the darkness.

The blizzard continued to rage and swept across the

moor burying everything in its path and the prison was soon cut off from the outside world. Sergeant Greaves knocked on the door and entered the Agent's office and as the door opened, the thick snow blew in around him.

'The road to Plymouth is blocked, sir. They won't be able to get any supplies through for a least a week,' he said, 'and the water's frozen solid.'

'You know what to do, Sergeant,' replied the Agent.

'Yessir!' he replied, as he pulled up the collar of his jacket and left.

As the blizzard continued to rage across the moor the sentry posts remained deserted as a strange silence enveloped the depot and surrounding moorland.

The snow was more than four foot deep when Sergeant Greaves almost unrecognizable, beneath the hat, scarf and raised collar of his jacket, made his way into Number Three Block. 'If you don't want to starve I need three volunteers to help me,' he said his voice muffled beneath the scarf.

'Help you? You must be joking,' mocked Ram Barley.

The Sergeant kicked his boots against the granite wall leaving huge lumps of snow and ice on the floor. 'That's fine.' He paused, 'but there's no more food,' he shouted threateningly.

He stood and waited as the moans and murmurs built to a crescendo.

'You're gonna leave us to starve is that it?' shouted Dylan Chipp.

'We have emergency rations,' replied the Sergeant. 'But if you don't want them, you *will* starve,' he said.

'There you are,' said Dylan as he turned and looked directly at the Sergeant. 'Idle threats, eh?' he mocked.

Sergeant Greaves pulled his scarf away from his mouth and the corner of his top lip rose slowly turning into a full smile. 'They ain't threats,' he said. 'The emergency rations need to be dug out,' he said firmly. 'You 'eard what I said...,' he stopped and with the atmosphere clearly strained, he waited. 'Let me tell you this. I <u>need</u> volunteers to help me. You can please yourselves, but if you want to die that's fine....' He took his time to look at each prisoner before he continued. 'But somehow I wonder if that's what you really want?' he said looking furtively around.

William Cole slipped out of his hammock and moved forward. 'I'll give you a hand,' he said.

'So will I,' said Benjamin Beck.

Peter Beck climbed down to join them. 'If we're gonna die we may as well be doing something useful,' he said glaring at Dylan Chipp.

'Ah,' spat a clearly embarrassed Dylan as he slid away and climbed awkwardly into his hammock.

The small group wrapped themselves in their blankets, pushed their way through those still standing and followed Sergeant Greaves out into the blizzard.

'Make sure you shut that door!' boomed Dylan as they left the block.

The Sergeant gave each of them a shovel and as the blizzard raged they slowly dug their way across the yard to the store room.

They forced the door open and staggered exhausted inside.

Sergeant Greaves lit an oil lamp which exposed the boxes and sacks stacked neatly against the far wall.

'Grab as much as you can carry and you can cook it outside yer block,' he said as he rubbed his freezing hands, stamped his boots and kicked off the new snow.

William, Benjamin and Peter rushed forward, grabbed at the boxes and sacks and made their way to the door but struggled to get out as prisoners from the other blocks staggered in to join them.

'Wait yer turn!' boomed Sergeant Greaves.

William Cole and Peter Beck cleared an area of snow and ice at the foot of the granite staircase outside of their block and while William returned to the slightly warmer prison block Benjamin chose to cook a stew of boiled mutton, potatoes and parsnips on a makeshift fire of wood, straw and bones. He spent several hours in the sub-zero temperatures and deep snow, whipped up by the bitter easterly wind, his thinly clad body protected only by a single blanket which he held around his body with his exposed left hand while he stirred the large pot with his right. His warm breath froze immediately it left his mouth leaving a crusty ice coating on his face, eye brows and any hair not covered by his woollen cap.

Marshall and Jeremiah finally served the hot mutton stew to the now starving inmates before retiring to their hammocks and endeavouring to keep their weak bodies warm while they dreamt of freedom.

In the semi-darkness, the prisoners continued to shiver, cough and moan relentlessly.

'Can it get much colder?' asked Ram Barley.

'Last year we had snow the whole winter,' said Ralph Etherington.

'Go to sleep, don't waste your energy,' shouted Jeremiah Hatch.

Two days later the sun shone for the first time in more than a week and the snow began to temporally thaw in the areas touched by its weak winter rays. The wretched and sickly prisoners shuffled around in the slush trying to find even the smallest of those areas where they could get even a little warmth.

''Nother day en der und I'd 'ave killed maself,' moaned Joshua Amos.

Benjamin Beck followed the Joshua around the yard and nodded his agreement as he rubbed the painful blackening index and fore finger on his left hand.

'Keep moving,' shouted a guard lowering his rifle and flashing his bayonet.

Benjamin's fingers continued to blacken and swell and a few days later an orderly escorted him into the infirmary and Doctor MacGrath amputated the two distorted frostbitten fingers.

'You're the lucky one,' said the Doctor as he stitched the second stub, which a few minutes earlier had been a rotting finger. 'I'd like a penny for every toe or finger I've amputated in 'ere,' said the Doctor in a matter of fact manner.

Benjamin gave him a puzzled look and then spoke.

'Lucky, I've just lost a couple of ma bloody fingers,' he growled.

The orderly piped up. 'Could've lost yer hand or yer ear,' he said. He paused and sniggered, 'or yer whole bleeding arm,' he said laughing nervously.

Doctor MacGrath fired him an angry look and the embarrassed orderly shuffled off.

'I could have saved them you know,' said Doctor MacGrath pointing at Benjamin's grossly disfigured fingers in the tray beside the operating table.

Benjamin looked at him quizzically before his face was suddenly transformed into a look of deep alarm. 'What?' he mouthed

The Doctor smiled and patted him gently on the shoulder. 'I'm sorry,' he said. 'I was a little premature in saying that.' He stopped to concentrate on bandaging the wound. 'At the moment...,' he paused to look up at Benjamin. 'It's only hear say from my contemporaries but I hear tell that Baron Dominique Larrey, Napoleon's surgeon general, has a new technique for treating frostbite.' He sighed. 'Let's just hope he has, we could do with it in here.'

෨)෬

ഇൽ Chapter ten ഇൽ

Captain Shortland and Sir Thomas Tyrwhitt sat and drank cider in a discreet corner of the Plume of Feathers.

'Well Captain, at last it's over,' whispered Sir Thomas Tyrwhitt.

'Over?' asked a surprised Captain Shortland.

'Aye, it is that, Captain. To be honest it hasn't come soon enough,' he sighed.

Sir Thomas raised his arms and waved across to the buxom young woman clearing the tables. 'Alice! Let's have more drinks over here,' he shouted before slamming his empty tankard onto the table.

He reflected. 'But I don't reckon they'll be going anywhere for quite sometime, quite sometime,' he said quietly.

A very drunk Captain Shortland staggered into his office

to find Doctor MacGrath completing a pile of death certificates.

'Well George, Sir Thomas has just me told we signed a peace treaty with the Yankees in Belgium on Christmas Eve,' he said.

'Thank God, Captain,' said a very relieved Doctor MacGrath. 'Look at this,' he said pointing at the death certificates in front of him. 'It can't come soon enough as far as I'm concerned,' he paused before continuing. 'I've done just about all I can with the meagre resources I have available to me in here,' he said, as he flicked through the certificates and shook his head.

Captain Shortland looked apprehensive and poured two large glasses of cognac passing the smallest to the Doctor.

'You don't seem too pleased about the news, Captain,' asked the Doctor.

'It's still not been ratified by London,' he replied.

The Doctor took a sip of his cognac and lit a cigar. 'Oh, I see.' He nodded slowly. 'Well at least in principle it's over, so I suppose we'll soon have an empty prison,' he said taking a huge drag on his cigar and coughing wildly. Finally catching his breath he was able to speak.

'It will change our lives, you know,' he said tapping the ash onto the floor.

'Don't be too sure about that George, if Napoleon carries on the way he is then we'll be full to the gunnels with Frenchies before you know it,' he said licking his lips reminiscing on his hunting jaunts. 'Come come, let's have another drink.'

The Doctor topped up his own glass and poured a full glass for Captain Shortland who emptied it with one huge gulp.

'Come on drink up let's have another of Squire Irwin's fine French cognac, made by an Englishmen no less,' said the Agent with a smile.

Some of the prisoners played football while others walked and talked in small groups. Robert Stapley kicked the ball hard over the inner wall and a guard threw it back almost immediately.

Ram Barley raced across the yard. 'It's over... the war's over... we're free... free!' he screamed finding it hard to get the words out.

Gradually the prisoners began to take notice.

'The war's over... yeah...,' they yelled uncontrollably.

There was great excitement as the word spread and

the other prisoners gradually began to spew out into the yard to join him.

The guards and militia were taken by total surprise and stood shocked and speechless as almost instantaneously the whole prison took on an unexpected transformation as scenes of elation, celebration and euphoria spread throughout the depot.

'I told you we'd beat the British bastards! Now we can get out of this shit hole... this vile place!' screamed Dylan Chipp.

Captain Shortland flanked by Doctor MacGrath and Sergeant Greaves walked out of his office and into the prison yard.

There was immediate silence as the American prisoners-of-war turned to listen.

'I can confirm what you have all been hearing. The war is officially over,' said Captain Shortland maintaining a stern look while he waved the letter above his head.

The prisoners whooped excitedly but soon realised that all is not well and the cheers quickly subsided.

'Is it right that the British lost the battle of New Orleans?' shouted Asha Adams.

The Captain hesitated. 'Yes... yes it is,' he stuttered speaking in an unusually subdued voice.

There were deafening cheers of jubilation.

He raised the letter higher in the air. 'I received this letter from Mr Beasly a few moments ago,' he said before lowering his head to read it.

He quoted: "An agreement has been reached between the British and American governments and we are making arrangements for all of our citizens to be repatriated."

There was absolute uproar and Dylan Chipp thinking he was unnoticed began to walk away from the other prisoners. 'Come on! We're free! It's over! What are you waiting for?' he screamed, waving his arms wildly as he made his way towards the Agent.

The prisoners continued to demonstrate their very special celebration.

Captain Shortland grabbed a rifle from the nearest guard and began to shake with rage as he dribbled and swayed, drunk and barely in control. He pointed the rifle menacingly at Dylan Chipp, glared at him before he aimed and fired. Dylan staggered across the yard and slumped to the ground at Captain Shortland's feet. He lay in the mud staring up at him, his crazed eyes displaying his pain and sheer terror.

The euphoria stopped abruptly.

There was total silence, everyone stood, rooted to the spot.

'I will confirm, the treaty was signed in Ghent, Belgium on the 24th of December 1814,' he said trying to complete the reading of the letter. He took a deep breath and forced himself to continue the reading. "Until the agreement is ratified and we can reach accord as to who is responsible for the cost of the repatriation of our most loyal citizens we are unable to confirm a date for their release." As he folded the letter he finished, "Signed Mister Rueben G Beasly... American Consul and Agent."

As he slipped the letter into the inside pocket of his jacket there was uproar and shouts of disbelief.

Then total silence.

The Agent coughed nervously and then in a loud voice continued. 'So you see... you will <u>all</u> be staying here for a while longer,' his last words were drowned out by the jeers and screams of disappointment and anger.

Captain Shortland pointed at Dylan Chipp lying prone in the mud.

'Take him away... and the rest of you get back to your cells,' he boomed.

The prisoner's tempers started to fray and the discontent quickly grew as they fought amongst themselves.

'If any of you are still considering escape... then I suggest that you think carefully. And anyone who even makes an attempt to leave this place will be hunted down,' screamed the Agent.

Sergeant Greaves made sure that Captain Shortland had finished before he barked his orders. 'Let's go! Get back to your cells... now!' he ordered cracking his whip indiscriminately.

The guards and militia fixed their bayonets and jabbed out blindly.

Dylan Chipp screamed out with pain and two militiamen stepped nervously forward and dragged him away to the infirmary.

The remaining guards moved slowly towards the prisoners and prodded them fiercely with their bayonets until they finally dispersed.

Hatred is the key

೫೦೧೪ Chapter eleven ೫೦೧೪

The peat fire cast eerie shadows across the wet flagstone floors of the Plume of Feather. The damp rose from the farmers' wet overcoats as the rain soaked fabric began to dry in the heat.

It was noisy and smoky but warm, respite from the cold moorland night.

Captain Shortland and Squire Irwin sat drinking cider at a table in a very dark and discreet corner.

'Captain, it will be spring in a few days. Can't we get some use out of these Yankees before they all kill each other or die with the pox?' asked the Squire.

'I don't know about that,' replied Captain Shortland as he screwed up his face in disagreement.

'Come, come Captain, these aren't like the stinking Frenchies. We can at least talk to the Yankees,' said the

Squire before taking a huge swig of his cider and emptying the tankard. 'And, they speak English....' He waved his arm in the air. 'Alice! Let's have some more cider over here,' he shouted drunkenly.

Captain Shortland looked at him sternly. 'That's why it's more difficult. Most of the Frenchies couldn't speak English so they couldn't hide that fact. With the Yankees it's very different.' He paused. 'They do speak English and if they get off the moor they'll be away to France or given the choice back to America,' he said.

He sucked at his empty pipe deep in thought. 'I dunno,' he said.

Alice walked across to the table carrying two tankards of cider and before she could place them on the table the Squire grabbed at her buttocks.

'Squire Irwin!' teased Alice with a girly giggle.

'I'll be seeing you later then, Alice?' whispered the Squire.

Alice winked at him and skipped off towards the bar.

'She's a good girl,' mumbled the Squire through his cider.

Shortland ignored him. 'Um... I'll give it some thought, Squire,' he replied.

Groups of prisoners stood around the yard and watched as the orderlies carried more dead prisoners out of the infirmary.

Sergeant Greaves leaned against the Agent's porch and looked the nearest prisoners up and down before finally walking towards them and cracking his whip. As soon as he had their undivided attention he pointed at those he had chosen. 'I want you... you and you. Stand over there,' he boomed. He looked another group up and down before pointing at each individual with his whip. 'You, stand over there.'

Peter Beck, Charles Blasden, Miles Longman and Ram Barley made there way nervously across to one side of the yard.

Sergeant Greaves slowly eyed another group before speaking. 'You, you...,' he paused. 'You two and them,' he said. 'Stand over there,' he ordered, using his whip to direct them.

Benjamin Beck, William Cole, Marshall Cunningham, Joshua Amos and Jeremiah Hatch made up the second group.

'That'll do, follow me,' he screamed as he strutted off towards the gates followed by the prisoners and their accompanying guards and militia.

He halted them near the outer wall and they were chained together in pairs before being marched beneath the granite arch to wait outside of the prison. They stood in silence and stared up at the words carved in the granite and looked around as it slowly dawned on them realised that for the first time in months they were in the outside world.

William Cole broke the silence. 'Some place eh?' he said.

'Whadever dem gut en store fer us, I's reckon we'm shou'd dry an' enjoy et,' said Joshua Amos.

'It's good be out of there, that's for sure,' said William.

'Speak for yourself,' said Marshall.

'Um…,' mumbled William.

A horse and cart pulled alongside them and a guard handed them picks and shovels.

'Who knows what they've got in store for us,' said William apprehensively.

Graham Sclater

൦൦ൔ

෨෮ Chapter twelve ෨෮

On the outskirts of Princetown, Randolph Cox, a young farm hand, tried desperately to repair a section of the damaged random stone walled new-take, containing cattle, sheep and horses. As he stepped forward to fix a temporary wooden barrier across the damaged granite wall another section disintegrated and crashed to the ground. As he jumped back the animals pushed and jostled each other nervously. Now in sheer panic and desperation they forced their way past Randolph and pushed through the gap in the wall and raced headlong towards Princetown.

The moorland town square was very busy, farmers stood in small groups while their wives chatted animatedly and children chased each other between the carriages and carts. Except for Sundays this was one of the few opportunities for them to play together and for their parents to catch up on any news.

An armed Marine, resplendent in his red tunic kept a close eye on Mara as she stood in the middle of the square and rested her arms on Priscilla's carriage and shared the latest gossip with each other. They laughed loudly but embarrassed at their unladylike outburst glimpsed around to establish if anyone had taken any notice.

On the opposite side of the square Thomas Irwin stood, unnoticed, in a doorway and stared longingly at Mara.

Peter Beck, Charles Blasden, Miles Longman, and Ram Barley, under the close scrutiny of two militiamen, worked nearby repairing the deep muddy ruts and furrows caused by the overloaded carts as they made their way to and from the depot.

Thomas Irwin looked up and saw the terrified cattle heading towards the square but turned away and walked off in the direction of the Duchy Hotel.

Peter Beck now saw the horses and cattle as they raced out of control towards the busy square bearing down on Mara and the Marine who were oblivious to the impending danger. Without a thought, Peter leapt between the animals and Mara pushing her and the Marine to the ground and safety beneath Priscilla's carriage.

The terrified animals thundered past them and out of the town square towards the open moor, leaving the devastation and sheer panic of screaming parents and crying children in their wake.

Peter lay motionless face down in the mud.

Mara and the Marine crawled out from beneath the carriage and rose slowly to their feet.

'Are you all right, ma'am?' asked the Marine nervously.

'Ye...s, I... I... think so,' she replied, clearly shaken.

Peter crawled out from beneath the carriage and tried to stand but was unable to do so and fell heavily back into the mud.

Mara knelt over him. 'You saved my life,' she murmured thankfully.

'And mine,' gushed the Marine.

Peter could see only a blurred image as the Marine reached out and helped him to his feet.

'Are you all right?' asked Mara, clearly concerned. She looked at him and waited for his reply.

'I can't see.' He gasped for air. 'Where are my glasses?' asked Peter his hands desperately feeling their way blindly through the thick mud.

Mara reached down and picked up the twisted mud encrusted frames and carefully rubbed the cracked glass before shaking her head to the Marine. 'I'm sorry but...,' she muttered, her voice still unable to hide her shock.

Peter reached out but before he could speak a militiaman senselessly jabbed a bayonet into his ribs and he fell back into the mud for the third time. 'Come on, get up! Get over there,' he snarled as he pointed his bayonet menacingly towards the other prisoners.

While Peter Beck lay in the mud Thomas Irwin ran across the square to join the crowd which had now gathered around Mara, Peter, the Marine and militiamen.

'Dear Mara, thank God you're safe,' said Thomas softly. 'It happened so quickly,' he looked around for agreement but there was none. 'I didn't see them coming,' he mumbled, as he reached across to Mara and made to hold her.

Mara ignored his words and pushed him aside.

His sister, Priscilla Irwin, the disgust clearly showing on her face, spat with anger.

'Thomas, why didn't you do something to help?' she screamed.

Her brother ignored her and turned away.

Ram Barley and Charles Blasden picked Peter up and manhandled him awkwardly towards the prison.

The militiamen clearly confused by the situation followed, their bayonets fixed and pointed half heartedly in the direction of the prisoners.

Mara looked on helplessly. 'Take care of him,' she mouthed, her whole body quivering with shock.

Still visibly distraught, the Marine assisted her, by holding her arm, as they picked their way through the crowd and deep mud.

Peter moaned in pain as an exhausted Ram Barley and Charles Blasden manhandled him awkwardly through the gates and into the infirmary.

'Put him on there and I'll have a look at him,' ordered Doctor MacGrath pointing at the well scrubbed operating table.

While the Doctor prepared his instruments his assistant looked Peter over and thoughtlessly tore at his bloodstained shirt and mud encased shoes.

Mara walked into the infirmary and stood at the door while the Doctor examined Peter's bleeding chest damaged by the broken protruding ribs before cutting through his trousers and concentrating on his crushed right leg.

The Doctor shook his head as he wiped away the blood and mud. 'I'm afraid, it's gonna have to come off,' he said as he reached for the saw.

Mara broke down. 'You can't!' she screamed.

Peter struggled to speak. 'Please no...,' he said shaking his head violently. 'Ram you gotta help me,' he begged.

Ram Barley, clearly agitated, approached the Doctor. 'Training and riding horses is all the boy knows. If you take 'is leg off you may as well kill him... right here! Right now!' he screamed.

'Surely, there's something you can do, Doctor MacGrath?' pleaded Mara. 'He saved my life. Please help him!' she screamed.

The Doctor looked at her in disbelief.

'He <u>did</u>!' she said taking a huge gulp of air. 'He saved my life,' she repeated softly.

Ram and Charles nodded in agreement their faces clearly affected by her heightened emotion.

'Give him a chance, doctor,' pleaded Ram Barley.

'Please... you gotta try,' begged Charles Blasden.

Doctor MacGrath looked at his assistant and then Mara before carefully selecting a scalpel from a battered ornate hardwood case. 'If that's what you want. I'm going to cut out some of this,' he said as he pulled back the shredded skin and poked at the damaged muscle and tissue. 'And stitch it up,' he said as he shook his head. 'Who knows?' he murmured.

He began by removing the damaged flesh and then stopped, his face displaying deep concern. 'But I'll tell you this, if gangrene sets in then it'll be him or this leg,' he said firmly.

'I'll come and see him every day,' sobbed Mara.

The Doctor looked up at Ram and Charles, smiled briefly and winked.

'I shall look forward to seeing you, Miss Shortland,' he said.

Ram Barley and Charles Blasden nearly choked with shock.

Peter flinched and looked across at them as they all

thought very different thoughts.

৪০০৪

ഔ Chapter thirteen ഔ

Sergeant Greaves, six militiamen and two guards marched Benjamin Beck, Thomas Johnson, Robert Stapley and a number of other prisoners out of the depot and along the moorland track towards the quarry.

Henrietta and Alex drove their flock of sheep across the narrow track and the prisoners stopped to let them pass. Benjamin Beck and Henrietta looked intensely at each other, immediately attracted to one another. Sergeant Greaves noticed and cracked his whip causing Benjamin to slip and fall down a gulley.

Robert looked nervously across at the Sergeant and climbed down to help Benjamin up onto the track. The two girls giggled as they walked off across the moor turning back every few yards to stare at the prisoners.

In the quarry Benjamin Beck, Thomas Johnson, Robert

Stapley and the other prisoners hacked at the huge granite rocks and made little impression -- the weeks in captivity and long periods of inactivity had left them weak and tired.

'Put some effort into it or you'll feel my leather!' screamed Sergeant Greaves blindly fingering his whip before cracking it threateningly.

The weary prisoners immediately stopped working and stood motionless.

The Sergeant clearly incensed by the display of defiance strode across to them and bellowed in their faces. 'Hurry up! I want that section broken out before we go back,' he screamed his face scarlet with rage. He turned and as he did so he took a huge breath before turning and cracking his whip like a man possessed. 'I said now! Get yerselves up and get on with it!' he bawled.

The guards and militiamen nervously fingered the triggers of their rifles.

Conscious of the heightening tension, the prisoners returned to their task of breaking out the granite boulders until late into the afternoon.

By now it was clear to Sergeant Greaves they were

near to physical exhaustion. He smirked at the guards and militia before screaming out his orders. 'Come on, let's go,' he bellowed. 'That's enough for today.' He turned and stepped towards each of them in turn and grinned widely. 'We've got tomorrow... and the next... and the next,' he paused. 'In fact... we've got as long as it takes,' he said slowly, relishing every word.

As they loaded their tools onto the cart and waited to begin the long and difficult journey back to the depot the Sergeant's words were still on their minds and showed clearly on their shocked faces.

The late afternoon sun was low in the cloudless sky as the prisoners stumbled across the moor. Their fatigue was clearly visible as they were marched through a wood until they reached a clearing and a crystal clear stream making its way down to join the river Dart.

They made to cross the clapper bridge but Sergeant Greaves bellowed his orders. 'Stay where you are,' he said.

They group stopped abruptly.

'Stinking Yankees could all do with a wash? Is that right, lads?' he shouted.

The loud cheers from the militiamen and guards

answered Sergeant's question. 'Strip off and get yerselves in there!' he screamed. He turned and smirked to the militiamen and guards. 'Get on with it, all of ya, strip off and get yer pale Yankee arses in there or you'll go in as you are,' he threatened.

The prisoners looked back at him in sheer disbelief.

'C'mon Sergeant, you don't really expect us to get into that?' pleaded Benjamin Beck.

'It's freezing in there,' moaned Robert Stapley.

Sergeant Greaves cracked his whip and the guards lowered there bayoneted rifles menacingly.

'You 'eard what I said,' he looked at them long and hard. 'Do it!' he said pausing and flexing his right arm. 'Now!' he screamed cracking his whip.

Henrietta and Alex were walking their sheep along the granite ridge when they heard the whip and anguished screams of the prisoners-of-war in the valley below.

Without a word they looked at each other and crawled through the heather and long grass towards the edge of the ridge and peered down. The sisters watched, shocked and wide-eyed at seeing the naked prisoners in the freezing water beneath them.

Their dogs barked excitedly and several sheep panicked and raced towards the edge, two of them sliding down the steep slope and falling into the water below.

Without thinking, the naked Benjamin and Thomas chased and caught the sheep and placed them unharmed on the bank on the opposite side of the river.

Benjamin looked up and noticed Henrietta and Alex peering down at him before they disappeared from view behind a boulder.

Sergeant Greaves cracked his whip wildly. 'Come on, get out of there and get dressed!' he ordered.

The prisoners made the futile attempt to dry themselves in the now biting easterly wind.

Henrietta turned to her younger sister. 'You stay 'ere and look after 'em,' she said pointing at the rest of the sheep.

She left Alex on the top of the ridge and climbed effortlessly down the rock face.

She grabbed the sheep and as she made to take the path she turned to Benjamin. 'Thank you, sir,' she said blushing.

Sergeant Greaves stood watching feeding his whip

through his thick fingers. 'Get away from her,' he boomed.

Benjamin ignored him and reached down, picked a primrose and handed it to the teenage girl.

As she was acknowledging him with a wide smile the whip cracked taking the flower from between her delicate fingers splitting it in two.

Benjamin lost his temper and raced towards Sergeant Greaves, and, as the guards pulled back the hammers on their rifles Robert and Thomas grabbed Benjamin and forcefully dragged him away.

'Let me go!' seethed Benjamin.

The Sergeant grinned widely, bent down and picked another primrose and passed it to Henrietta.

'Thank you, Sergeant Greaves, it's very nice,' she lied.

As soon as Benjamin saw this he renewed his efforts to break away from Robert and Thomas but with considerable effort they managed to hold him firm.

The Sergeant smiled and turned to tease Benjamin. 'Thank you, Henrietta,' he said. He clearly found it hard to pay any sort of compliment to anyone and blushed as he spoke. 'It's as pretty as you are,' he said flatteringly.

Henrietta turned and as she left picked up the two

pieces of primrose, climbed the slope, dropped the whole flower and turned back and smiled at Benjamin.

Sergeant Greaves immediately went berserk cracking his whip uncontrollably. 'Let's go!' he screamed wildly. 'Get a move along there!'

The remainder of the journey was torturous as the Sergeant forced the prisoners to make the journey at breakneck speed causing many of them to slip and injure themselves on the rough terrain.

Benjamin Beck and his fellow prisoners finally made . their way through the prison gates and into the yard.

'Wait there!' bellowed Sergeant Greaves overflowing with anger.

'What the hell's he doing now?' mumbled Benjamin.

The Sergeant suddenly flipped cracked his whip and ensnared Benjamin's leg. 'Take him away!' he screamed.

Several guards rushed forward and grabbed Benjamin and dragged him towards the *cachot*.

Henrietta and Alex aided by their dogs chased the sheep into their pen and walked towards the cottage.

Alex looked up at her sister and gave her a wide grin.

'Do you love 'im?' she teased.

''Course I don't,' blushed Henrietta.

Throughout their evening meal Henrietta sat in silence and played with her food.

'What's up with you tonight, Henrietta?' asked her father.

'She's got a boyfriend,' blurted out Alex.

'Have yer now?' said Harold Thomson. 'It's about time. I could do with a 'and around the farm… and in me workshop.' He placed his fork on the table and reflected. 'I won't always be around,' he said teasing them.

''Ee's a prisoner at the depot ya know,' gushed Alex.

'What?' exclaimed her father. 'A Yankee prisoner…?' he finished his dinner. 'What the hell are they doin' on the moor?' he asked himself.

Alex nodded while Henrietta kicked out at her.

Henrietta lay on her bed, held the two pieces of the primrose between her fingers, and tried to remember everything about the day. She opened a book and carefully laid the two pieces of primrose between the pages and closed it. She kissed the book and pulled it tight against her chest.

'You do, I know you do,' teased Alex.

Hatred is the key

෯)෬

❧ **Chapter fourteen** ❧

Marshall Cunningham, Joshua Amos, Jeremiah Hatch and young Sylas, worked in the copse at the edge of the garden chopping and sawing fallen branches and stacking them neatly at the edge of the garden. William Cole, Henry Sterling, Miles Longman and Dylan Chipp were cutting back overgrown shrubs and removing smaller pieces of granite from the moor and carrying it to the perimeter of the vast lawn. They were chained in pairs at the ankle and this restricted their movement and any chance of escape.

Thomas and Priscilla Irwin cantered onto the estate and down the gravel drive towards the working prisoners.

William Cole looked on and drooled as Priscilla trotted past him.

Jeremiah Hatch dug him in the ribs. 'You're wasting your time even thinking about it. She's a lady....' He paused. 'Wouldn't look at you twice,' he smirked and continued, 'even if you were a free man,' he said.

'I can dream can't I?' retorted William Cole.

The riders stopped briefly and while Joshua and Jeremiah both stared at the beautiful young woman, William clenched his fists and glared at Thomas.

'I'm more interested in killin' 'im. Don't forget....' He stood and screamed out uncontrollably. 'He killed our Captain in cold blood!' He tightened his fists and screwed his face in anger.

Thomas whipped his horse viciously and followed closely by Priscilla rode off towards the stables. The militiamen raced across to William and lashed out at him indiscriminately with their rifles knocking him to the ground and kicking him.

Dylan Chipp and Marshall Cunningham carried armfuls of logs into the barn and fell exhausted onto the straw. Marshall felt something in his back and pushed the straw away to reveal a clay flask. He pushed away more straw and found two more.

They each opened a flask, smelt the contents

cautiously and simultaneously took huge swigs followed by several more before falling back into the straw. They lay and smiled to each other in a semi-drunken stupor.

'This tastes expensive,' slurred Dylan Chipp as the alcohol took effect.

'Anything would taste expensive after the months in that place,' said Marshall.

'Maybe,' replied Dylan taking yet another slug of the alcohol. 'Surely we can get away from here?' he slurred.

'No way,' replied Marshall. 'I don't want to end up like that Frenchie, ripped to bits by them hounds,' he said, as he remembered the day they arrived at the depot.

'I don't see why not,' said Dylan Chipp. 'If we're gonna do it, then it has to be soon,' he said taking another gulp from the flask.

They rejoined the group ensuring for the rest of the day that they kept well away from the guards who would have certainly smelt the cognac on their breath.

The following day the prisoners sat under the trees at the edge of the large garden and waited.

'We ain't going nowhere, can't we have these things off?' asked Dylan.

'We'll be able to get more work done if we didn't,'

said Marshall.

The guards conversed and after several minutes of discussion unlocked the manacles and removed them.

'They go back on before we leave 'ere,' said the militia sergeant.

Collectively, the prisoners nodded their agreement.

The militiamen and guards sat near the main house concentrating their efforts on gorging themselves on the delicious food supplied by the Squire's cook.

Marshall Cunningham looked around, closed his eyes and nodded slowly.

The prisoners-of-war waiting for the agreed signal suddenly sprang into action and made a dash through the copse towards the moor. The Marines and militiamen were caught totally unawares and it was several seconds before they were able to collect their rifles, firing haphazardly in the direction of the escaping prisoners before making a token pursuit and chasing after them.

William Cole reached the edge of the estate but tripped and fell heavily.

The guards immediately grabbed him and beat him before dragging him back to the lawn.

In the mayhem Marshall Cunningham, Joshua Amos,

Jeremiah Hatch, Miles Longman, Henry Sterling and Dylan Chipp managed to get onto the moor and disappear from view hiding amongst the bracken and gorse.

Squire and Thomas Irwin rode in from Tavistock to witness the chaos as the militiamen and Marines were deciding what they should do next and who should do it.

Realising that the prisoners had escaped Thomas hung back nervously.

'What the hell is going on?' snarled the Squire through his gritted teeth.

'They've escaped, sir,' replied the nearest guard.

The Squire looked down at the injured William Cole. 'I can take care of him, he said. 'Don't let any of them get away. Shoot 'em if you have to,' he fumed.

The Squire now turned his attention to Thomas. 'You go with them,' he said. Still eying the cowering prisoner he lowered his voice. 'And be careful,' he said softly.

Thomas nodded and reluctantly raced off across the moor followed by a handful of the militia and guards taking up the rear on foot.

Priscilla Irwin sat at the window and had watched the escape attempt unfold and smiled to herself pleased that

Hatred is the key

William had not gone out onto the wild moor.

As the night drew in Marshall Cunningham, Joshua Amos, Jeremiah Hatch, Miles Longman, Henry Sterling and Dylan Chipp wandered aimlessly in the thick mist. Joshua tripped and fell into a gully, badly cutting his leg, twisting his ankle and damaging his arm and shoulder. Marshall followed cautiously several yards behind and without acknowledging Joshua he passed him and broke into a run before disappearing into the darkness.

Dylan, Miles and Henry veered off in another direction but disregarding the treacherous terrain they soon tripped and Dylan and Henry fell heavily into the bog and began to sink.

'Get us out of here!' screamed Dylan Chipp.

'I can't, I'm sinking too,' moaned Henry Sterling in a desperate high pitched voice.

Miles continued to make good progress and was already several yards ahead. He hesitated when he heard the cries, looked back and then continued.

'Miles! Come on man, get me out!' screamed Henry, his voice fading into the night.

Miles stopped again and hearing the continuing pleas for help looked back into the darkness and after a few moments of careful consideration walked slowly back towards them.

'Come on there boy... get me out... help your old friend, that's a good fella,' said Dylan Chipp, feigning sincerity.

Miles stood glaring at him.

'Miles! Over here! Come on Miles, I'm gonna die,' he took a deep breath and began to beg again. 'Over here,' pleaded Dylan carefully choosing every word to coax the only person who could save his life. It had the desired effect and Miles walked out of the night took stock of the situation and slid along on his stomach, reached out and slowly pulled Henry out of the bog.

'Thank you,' muttered Henry. 'Thank you very much Miles, you are a true gentleman. You could have left me to die... thank you... thank you...,' he repeated continuously.

'Mmm... mm... Miles come on, boy,' he stuttered. 'How about me?' screamed Dylan Chipp sinking ever deeper into the bog.

He struggled to breathe as the dark foul water entered his mouth.

'Stop struggling or you'll sink deeper,' shouted

Henry.

Miles stood looking down at his owner and remembered his years as a slave and the vicious treatment this man had meted out to him. Carefully choosing every word he mimicked Charles Blasden's voice and in a high pitched tone he spoke. 'Save yerself, if you can... ma Lord,' he said before turning and running off into the night.

Dylan now focused his attention on Henry

'Come on, Henry, get me out!' he screamed.

Henry Sterling stood shivering and shocked at the edge of the bog unsure of where he was or what was happening to him.

'Come on, man, just get me out!' screamed a very desperate Dylan Chipp. 'Come on! Help m...,' he mouthed as he disappeared beneath the dark peat soaked quagmire.

Henry slowly came to his senses and searched through the bracken and gorse until he found a suitable branch. He lay down on his stomach and edged anxiously towards Dylan.

'That's it... that's it, you're nearly there,' coaxed Dylan.

Henry stretched the final few inches until Dylan could reach the branch. He grabbed at it pulled himself from the treacherous bog and stood shaking beside his rescuer.

'There you are, we made it,' said a much relieved Dylan.

He looked out into the darkness. 'As for that black bastard....' He shivered uncontrollably. 'I'll have 'im flogged when I catch up with him,' he cursed before taking a deep breath. He turned his head in disgust at the revolting smell of the rotting bog and removed his jacket. He screwed it up and forcefully squeezed it out but as he did so his elbow brushed against the trembling Henry Sterling and accidentally pushed his rescuer.

Henry fell back into the deep bog and looked up to Dylan shaking his head in absolute terror.

'It's your turn to help me now, Dylan,' begged Henry.

Dylan glared back at him.

Henry's face conveyed his sheer panic as he screamed out. 'Dylan surely you will help me?' begged the drowning prisoner. He took a deep gasp and screamed out again. 'Have you no compassion, man!'

Dylan made no attempt to help him, instead he stood

and lacking any sign of emotion watched in silence as Henry Sterling took his last breath before disappearing beneath the bog. His eye patch floated to the surface, the only marker left of his previous existence.

Mara pushed her food around the plate. 'One of the Americans saved my life today,' she said quietly.

'I heard about it,' replied her father swallowing hard. 'Calling them Americans are we now?' he asked. 'They're our enemies for God sake,' he raged.

'Well... I don't like how you and Greaves refer to them,' she said defensively.

Her father put down his knife and glared hard at her his eyes staring into her very soul.

'Yankees, that's what they are... Yankees! Calling them by a different name won't change what or who they are,' he said forcefully.

Mara nodded her agreement. 'All right, Yankees,' she replied softly. She looked directly at her father before she spoke. 'Can I visit him in the infirmary?' she asked lowering her voice.

'Who is he?' enquired her father taking a massive gulp of his wine.

'I don't know his name,' she lied.

Her father lit a cigar and blew huge clouds of smoke across the table. 'I don't see why not,' he said swallowing the rest of the wine before pouring himself another glass. 'According to George MacGrath he's in a real bad way,' he said knowingly before stabbing the last piece of beef with his knife and pushing it past the cigar and into his smoke filled mouth.

❧ Chapter fifteen ❧

There was a strained silence in the Squire's drawing room as everyone contemplated what had happened and how Captain Shortland might react to the news.

Priscilla sat near the fire while Squire Irwin paced the floor, taking huge gulps of cognac as he walked. He finally snapped angrily and turned to face William Cole before he staggered across to him.

The Squire looked directly into William's face. 'They must be mad!' he screamed. 'There's no way any of them will get off the moor alive. Shortland will kill 'em all when he catches up with 'em,' he smiled a drunken smile. 'And, mark my words... he will....'

William Cole couldn't remain silent any longer and interrupted the Squire. 'If, he catches them, sir,' he retorted.

'Who spoke to you?' replied the Squire curtly before pouring yet another cognac and smirking to himself as he slipped into his favourite arm chair. 'In a way, boy, I suppose you were the lucky one,' he grinned, pushing himself deep into his favourite chair.

Priscilla coughed nervously before speaking. 'Father, he wasn't trying to escape. He was chasing them,' she said.

'What?' uttered her father. 'Was he really? Do you expect me to believe that nonsense?' he sniggered.

'That's right, sir,' said William Cole. 'I was trying to catch them. Mmm... uh to persuade them not to run.' He looked across at Priscilla and smiled. 'You're right, sir. They must be totally mad to even attempt an escape,' he said.

The Squire thought before answering. 'All right,' he pondered sipping at his cognac. 'But if I hear any different I'll personally have you flogged,' he said.

Priscilla seized the moment. 'Father, can William come here again?' she asked softly.

'What did you say?' asked a stunned Thomas Irwin.

She turned to face her brother and glared at him.

Priscilla now turned to her father. 'Well, he's no threat

and how can he possibly go anywhere like that?' she asked, 'he can hardly walk let alone run.' She said, pointing at William's bleeding legs.

'Perhaps,' replied her father.

Priscilla smiled while her brother fired a furious look across at her and beat his clenched fists on the arms of the leather chair.

The Squire pushed himself awkwardly out of his chair and coughed loudly. 'Yankee, you'd best get something done to them legs,' he scoffed before staggering drunkenly out of the room.

The snow continued to fall heavily and within an hour it had formed deep drifts across the moor making it impassable.

Sergeant Greaves hammered on Captain Shortland's door before bursting in on him.

The Captain was drinking the last few drops of what had been an almost full a bottle of rum.

'We've lost the prisoners, sir,' the Sergeant blurted out excitedly.

'Lost? How can you lose...?' he thought to himself, 'six prisoners?'

'They escaped from the working party at Squire

Irwin's estate, sir,' he said.

Captain Shortland sat back in his chair and lit another cigar. 'Leave 'em 'til the morning,' he said leaning deeper into his chair and blowing huge clouds of smoke across the room. After reflecting on the matter he continued. 'They'll be begging to come back by then,' he said. 'In this weather they'll be easier to track. Let's leave 'em to freeze to death and if any of 'em are still alive the dogs can have 'em,' he said, trying to squeeze the last few drops from the already empty bottle.

'Yessir!' answered the Sergeant before leaving the office and walking out into the raging blizzard.

Joshua Amos struggled across the moor, tripping on the gorse and stumbling on the large rocks. It began to snow heavily and with visibility restricted to a few feet he crawled into the dense Bellever wood, set deep within the estate of Captain Sleep. He fell asleep briefly and as the last of the snow clouds blew across the night sky the full moon cast bright flashes of light through the trees. He awoke in excruciating pain, pulled himself to his feet and dragged himself towards the edge of the forest.

He leaned against a large fir tree and the thick powdery snow fell onto his head and shoulders, clogging his already matted hair to his head and freezing in seconds.

He tried to brush it from his already wet clothes and as he looked out onto the glistening landscape he shook with a combination of pain, cold and foreboding.

Joshua partially closed his tired eyes, screwed up his face and rapidly became accustomed to the bright reflections of the moon across the white surreal landscape. He summoned his strength, decided on a direction and grabbed at a fallen branch, removed the smaller pieces and fashioned a walking stick. He pushed himself away from the tree and struggled through the deep drifts, the light wind that always followed snow blew across his frozen face. In an attempt to avoid the invisible dangers hidden deep beneath the snow he used his stick as a probe thrusting it deep into the drifts before moving cautiously forward. He continued for several hours and as the sky lightened with the impending dawn he noticed smoke billowing up into the sky a short distance from him. He took a deep pained breath and dragged his damaged body painfully across the frozen landscape towards the smoke. As he got nearer he noticed a flickering light in the window of the isolated cottage.

Joshua made one final effort and reached the cottage. He sneaked around the granite building until he reached the illuminated window, crouched down and peered through the shutters.

The only light came from a candle which flickered on a table near the window and the burnt out embers in the fire place. A man was asleep in a chair near the fire and younger woman sat at the table mixing coloured liquids that boiled and bubbled in front of her.

He pulled back suddenly and slipped, falling heavily against the pile of logs stowed along the wall.

Hearing the crashing logs the man awoke and jumped from his chair causing it to smash against the table and the woman to react with a start, her flaying arms smashing some of the glass phials and spilling the bubbling liquid onto the flagstone floor.

'What de?' she cursed angrily.

The man looked across at the woman, put his finger to his mouth, lit a lantern and made his way warily towards the door. He opened the door wide enough to enable him to push the lantern outside and moved it from side to side illuminating the immediate area.

He saw nothing and began to close the door.

'Please 'elp ma, massa,' moaned an exhausted Joshua Amos. '…'and ma over if ya wunt… jut git me outta dis,' he pleaded.

The man hearing the pleas for help opened the door wide, stepped outside and cautiously made his way through the snow until his lantern lit up the escaped prisoner's terrified and pained face. The man leaned forward to help Joshua but he resisted his assistance pulling his arms away as he made a futile attempt to stand.

'Do 'ee want us to 'elp 'ee or not?' cursed the man, through his frozen breath. He forcefully dragged the terrified and exhausted stranger uncertainly towards the door.

'Can 'ee listen to 'n squaalin,' shouted the man. 'Give us an 'and will 'ee!'

Joshua now slipped into a state of unconsciousness.

'Look at 'th great gawk, 'ee be a-veered 'o a little ole appledrane,' he said.

The young woman appeared at the door and after furtively looking around helped the man to manhandle the stranger into the cottage, sliding him along the floor and propping him against the chair in front of the fire.

'Th' zo 'n zo be praaper tizzicky,' said the man.

The woman nodded and cleaned the coloured liquid from the flagstone floor while the man raked the wood embers, and, after carefully selecting the smallest and driest logs, he placed them on the fire.

Joshua remained propped awkwardly against the chair but as the logs ignited, the heat slowly caused the ice to melt and run down his black cheeks. The Stranger gradually regained consciousness and as he shivered uncontrollably his teeth cut deep into his bottom lip. He licked at the warm blood as it ran down his chin and tried to wipe the residue away but unable to control his still frozen hands and coordinate his movements his efforts were futile.

The dry logs suddenly burst into flames, illuminating every part of the room.

As the ice thawed on his encrusted eye lids and the ice cold water ran down his pock marked face he was gradually able to open his eyes and focus, and take in his surroundings.

Dried toads, frogs, rats and animals heads filled every corner; small cages held live rats and mice and in a glass tank frogs and newts made exhaustive and futile attempts to escape by clawing their way up the glass and falling down again.

Witches effects were everywhere.

The woman turned to face him and for the first time he noticed her disfigured face.

Although Joshua desperately wanted to escape he couldn't move his faculties temporarily destroyed. At that moment a look of abject terror was etched into his already pained expression and now absolutely petrified he lost all control and pissed himself.

'There's nothin' to worry 'bout,' whispered the woman reassuringly as she bent down beside him and wiped the blood and remaining ice from his fear stricken face.

'Let's get them clathers off 'im, or 'ee'll die of pneumonia,' said the man flashing a concerned look towards the woman.

'But 'ee can't stay there,' said the woman pointing at the roaring fire.

Unable to speak, Joshua looked at her and asked her a question with his eyes.

She looked at him and understood what he was

unable to say.

She smiled before speaking. 'No, I meant yer'll get too 'ot if 'ee stays that close to the fire and that's bad fer 'ee,' she said and continued clearly anxious, 'it'll put fever in yer blood.'

The man smiled at him and left the room to return with a metal bath, which he placed in front of the now roaring fire and filled it with water from the kettle hanging above the fire mixing it with cold water from the well.

As the man stooped to fill the bath Joshua noticed his severely hunched back for the first time and stiffened.

Without warning the woman reached for a razor sharp knife and lunged towards him. With exacting precision she sliced through his wet clothes, tore them from his emaciated and scared body and threw them onto the fire to sizzle before bursting into flames.

Noticing his terrified reaction the woman spoke softly. 'You be in the best place, so don't 'ee worry,' she said.

Joshua didn't hear her. His fear turned to abject horror.

Instead he sat wide eyed and dumb struck, his eyes

darting wildly between the man and woman before staring blindly at his clothes burning on the fire.

She shook her head knowingly, moved close to him and smiled before speaking in a voice of pure velvet. 'Us told 'ee not to worry.' She smiled again. 'Us'll look after 'ee,' she said. 'Me and me brother, Phinias, 'arm good at what us do's,' she said proudly.

Joshua began to relax and nodded enthusiastically.

'That's better,' said the man looking across at his sister. 'As you 'eard, I'm Phinias and me sister's name is, Giselle.'

Phinias smiled at her proudly and she grinned at Joshua.

'What's yer name?' asked Phinias with genuine interest in his voice.

Joshua gave him a quizzical look.

Giselle tapped Joshua on the shoulder. 'Don't 'ee worry,' she said. 'We can see 'ee be frum the depot,' she looked across to her brother. 'It don't bother us 't all... ain't that right Phinias?' asked Giselle.

Phinias nodded his agreement.

Joshua swallowed hard and licked at his lips before speaking. 'I be Joshua Amos, frum Number Three Block,' he replied. He picked the dried blood from the corners of his mouth and continued. 'I wuz a slave an da *Libertine*,' he said and paused suddenly, '...captured by *ya* British....'

He looked at them and continued slowly. 'In a...,' he reflected and wiped his tearful eyes. 'In a bloody battle,' he said sadly, his wide eyes flooding with tears.

Sensing his wretchedness Phinias interrupted him. 'Cum on, let's get 'ee in that there bath and we can clean them wounds and 'elp 'ee git better,' he said.

'We'll soon 'ave 'ee better,' she said reassuringly. 'Just you zee.'

Under cover of the cloudy night and shrouded in thick mist a hooded figure carrying a wooden cask made its way across the expansive courtyard and entered the stable block. The horses kicked out nervously as the figure pulled back the straw, laid the cask in one of the stalls and partially covered it before leaving unnoticed.

Hatred is the key

ഇൗൽ

✂ Chapter sixteen ✂

The snow was thawing fast when Captain Shortland arrived at the Squire Irwin's estate with his dogs and a group of militiamen and Marines to join the hunt for the escapees.

Squire Irwin and Thomas were already mounted on their horses and Priscilla sat in the carriage with her mother.

The Captain touched his hat. 'Good morning, Mrs Irwin, Priscilla,' he said courteously.

'Good morning, Captain,' replied Mrs Irwin.

'Are you riding with us, ma'am... miss?' he asked.

'Certainly not, Captain,' replied Priscilla curtly.

'We're going into Tavistock,' replied Mrs Irwin trying to defuse the obvious tension.

Priscilla looked nervously at the dogs, their fur already thick with mud, as they ran around excitedly in the deep brown slush. 'Captain, do you think they are really necessary?' she asked. 'After all... the American prisoners <u>are</u> human beings.'

The Captain moved nearer to the carriage clearly affected by her comment.

'Human! They're not human, ma'am. If you saw what I have to look at every day you couldn't possibly say that,' he said shaking with anger. 'Come Squire! Thomas! Let's catch 'em all before lunch. Dead or alive!' he screamed as he dug his boot heels deep into his horses flank and raced off followed by the hounds.

'I'll wager a guinea, I bag the first Yankee,' shouted the Squire as he chased after Captain Shortland.

The dogs barked excitedly having already picked up the scent and Captain Shortland raced across the moor, followed by the baying hounds while Squire Irwin and Thomas tried to keep up with him.

Many of the dogs became extremely excited and ran towards a jagged outcrop of rock. As they reached it Dylan Chipp jumped out, grabbed the injured Miles Longman and pulled him up. They both stood shivering, wet, hungry and very tired.

'Here he is!' shouted Dylan Chipp frantically waving

his arms.

The dogs, smelling blood, snapped at the slave's already ripped and lacerated legs, while others jumped at his arms, their teeth digging deep into his already pained and bleeding flesh.

Miles totally shocked by Dylan Chipp's action ignored the pain, glared at him and pushed his arms away. 'Next dime, I will kill ya,' he threatened as he gritted his teeth in unbounded rage.

Ignoring Dylan Chipp's shouts Captain Shortland fired off his instructions to the nearest Marines. 'You stay with these two. I'll be back with the others. They can't be far away now,' he said.

He looked at the Squire. 'And that's a guinea you owe me,' he said before racing off once again followed closely by his yapping dogs.

Marshall Cunningham had taken refuge a short distance away in a warrener's shelter but the dogs soon found him and it wasn't long before he was tethered to Miles and Dylan.

Asha Adams ran into the market square. 'There's been a breakout!' he shouted gasping for breath.

Everyone stopped and there was a surreal silence

while they waited for confirmation.

'I said,' he spun around and looked at his fellow prisoners before allowing a wide grin to fill his emaciated face. 'I said...,' he paused, '...there's been a breakout!' he screamed. 'They've escaped... they've escaped...' he repeated.

As if on cue the whole prison erupted into thunderous shouts, whoops and whistles of celebration.

'Let's hope they give 'emselves up before Shortland finds 'em,' mumbled Charles Blasden biting at his top lip and wiping the blood with his filthy left hand.

As always the prison market was bustling with prisoners but this time they talked excitedly about the escape, while the militia and guards looked to spend their allowances.

Henrietta and Alex stood behind their stall selling home made cakes and wool.

Robert Stapley and Thomas Johnson walked past their stall.

Henrietta recognized them and attracted their attention. 'Is 'ee all right?' she asked nervously.

'Who?' they asked simultaneously.

Alex blurted out unthinkingly.

'Your friend....' She paused and nudged her sister, 'the Yankee who gave her the primrose,' she said.

'Well, your *friend*...,' he shot her an angry look, 'the Sergeant, as you call him, had him thrown into the *cachot*. If you think that's all right?' he said sarcastically.

'Friend? *Cachot*? What did 'ee do, sir?' she asked.

'Maybe you should ask the Sergeant,' said Robert gritting his teeth and seething with anger.

'Your friend... remember?' interrupted Thomas.

'The evil bastard was jealous, surely you could see that? That's why he put him in there,' said Robert.

He waited for a response. There was none.

He continued, 'Benjamin didn't deserve that.'

'Benjamin?' repeated Henrietta as she looked in the direction of the *cachot*. 'Benjamin,' she said softly, as she smiled and repeated his name for the third time.

Thomas Johnson moved towards her and whispered in her ear. 'He'll be fine,' he nodded, 'that one can look after himself that's fer sure.'

'I hope you be right,' she said.

In the darkest and most discreet area of the market Phinias and Giselle stood behind their stall. They displayed varying sized bottles of different coloured liquid, pieces of bone, coloured stones and glass phials containing powders of all colours, dried rats and frogs.

Two guards walked up to their stall, made to inspect the dried creatures and muttered to each other before speaking out. 'What do you evil, ugly bastards think you're doing here?' asked one of them.

'If that's shits any good why 'aven't ya used 'em yerselves,' asked the other with a snigger before laughing loudly as he walked away.

Ram Barley waited for the guards to leave and made to speak to Giselle.

She spoke to him before he opened his mouth. ''Ave 'ee vaught blid?' she asked.

Ram looked at her but was unable to speak.

She smiled knowingly and motioned to him to join her behind her stall. Nervously he moved towards her and she pulled out a milking stool.

She placed her hands on his shoulders and shouted to Phinias who was serving a black prisoner. ''Ee've got vaught blid?'

Phinias nodded to her and returned to weigh the green powder. He placed it in a clean piece of white linen, folded it carefully and handed it to the Negro.

Phinias lowered his head to the prisoner, smiled and gently touched his shoulder before turning to assist Giselle.

'I can 'elp 'ee,' she said in a soft velvet voice. 'Sit 'ee down 'ere.'

She pushed Ram gently onto the stool and smiled at him again before turning to check her phials, powders and potions. She carefully selected beeswax, sulphur and a little British oil and measured it before handing it to Phinias. She whispered her instructions to him and he proceeded to crush the ingredients into a paste in a pestle and mortar. When he was satisfied with the texture he handed it to his sister who placed it in the centre of a small clay tile.

Ram Barley sat in silence with his back to them as the unbearable pain continued to rage inside his head.

Giselle leaned forward and swung a piece of crystal tied to a cord rhythmically from side to side in front of Ram until he closed his eyes and she was able to open his mouth without pain.

Phinias fashioned a small cone from a piece of rat skin, lit the mixture and handed it to Giselle. She placed the cone over the smoke and pointed it at the hollow and inflamed wisdom tooth deep in Ram Barley's swollen mouth. She continued to hold it there until the mixture had burnt itself out before handing it to Phinias and nodding with satisfaction.

She stood behind Ram and gently massaged his neck until he opened his eyes twisted his head around and gave her a look of sheer euphoria.

''Ee needs to get that out of thee mouth,' she said.

He didn't understand and she gently touched his swollen cheek.

Ram pulled his head back, coughed loudly and spat the puss and blood onto the dried mud.

''As betta,' she said, smiling with satisfaction.

He licked his dry mouth and lips and coughed gently before speaking. 'Thank you very much... I couldn't stand it much longer... I felt like cutting me own throat...,' he said.

She smiled back at him and handed him a flask of water.

'There's no need for that, sir' she said. 'That got 'ee now,' she said. 'That's just three pennies, sir.'

While Ram was paying Phinias she whispered in his ear. 'Be you a friend of Joshua...? Joshua Amos?' she asked in little more than a whisper.

Ram looked surprised.

'Yeah,' he said guardedly.

'He be safe,' she mouthed placing her finger in front of her lips.

'How is he?' he gushed excitedly.

'He be bad but...,' she said, her voice fading.

His face suddenly changed. 'What?' he asked.

Giselle smiled at him. 'He'll get better. Don' 'ee worry,' she said.

'I'm sure he will,' he said rubbing his swollen cheek gently.

Ram looked at her and slowly his face broke into the widest grin. 'Thank you ma'am... thank you very much,' he said.

Giselle looked around and made to pass him a note. At first he hesitated but after realizing what was happening acknowledged her with a nod, took the note and slid it inside his jacket before disappearing into the crowd.

'I didn't ask 'is name,' she said looking out across the market.

'It don't matter, we'll see 'im again,' said Phinias

confidently.

They carefully packed their phials, powders and potions, dismantled their stall loaded their mule and left with the other traders.

The prison yard soon heaved with prisoners playing football and other games in the bright sunny afternoon.

The gates opened and the barking dogs raced in followed closely by Captain Shortland while staggering behind him tied to each other were the exhausted prisoners.

There was absolute silence.

The prisoners-of-war watched as the recaptured prisoners were dragged ignominiously into the depot.

Although clearly injured Miles Longman and Marshall Cunningham looked pleased to be back while lagging far behind were the dejected figures of William Cole and Dylan Chipp.

'No one escapes from me!' screamed an arrogant Captain Shortland. 'Get these bastards into the *cachot*, before I have 'em flogged. The rest of you get back to your cells,' he said pausing briefly before raising his head proudly. He let out a bloodcurdling scream that reverberated around the depot. '<u>Now!</u>'

Dylan made a futile gesture as the four of them were pushed and prodded with bayonets and rifle butts but realising it was pointless gave in and moved off towards the *cachot*.

The Captain coughed loudly to attract everyone's attention. He waited for total silence before he ceremoniously pulled the eye patch from his pocket and held his trophy high in the air. 'I believe this belonged to a...' he paused as his audience gasped loudly. 'Henry Sterling, no less,' he boomed, ensuring his voice was heard by everyone gathered in the yard. '...he's dead... dead!' he screamed proudly before he sniggered and turned, throwing the eye patch into the air to be ripped apart by the dogs before it reached the thawing mud and ice.

The recaptured prisoners stood rooted to the spot as the Agent's horse trotted towards his office before he dismounted.

'What about Joshua?' shouted young Sylas.

The Agent turned slowly and smirked broadly savouring the moment before he replied. 'Dead!' he paused, 'I already told yer... they're both dead,' he boasted.

Number Three Block was unusually quiet with an air of despair. Ram Barley moved unnoticed across the block and passed the note to Jeremiah Hatch who was swinging in his hammock with his eyes closed and singing softly to himself.

He could dream; sometimes.

Jeremiah struggled to read in the poor light tilting the paper from side to side reading each word and rereading it before sliding out of his hammock. 'He's not dead! Joshua made it!' he shouted and jumped excitedly around. 'He made it! He made it!' he continued.

'Thank God… I've been praying for him,' said Asha Adams as the block suddenly erupted.

Sir Thomas Tyrwhitt and his guests sat around the huge dining table at Tor Royal. The main course was almost finished and the wine flowed freely. Uneaten dishes of food and half finished plates filled the table.

'So Captain, have you now caught all the escapees?' asked Sir Thomas Tyrwhitt sipping at his wine.

'All except one of 'em…,' said Captain Shortland sipping at his wine. 'I'm sure he'll turn up in a day or so… begging us to let him in,' he lied.

Priscilla could hold her tongue no longer and spoke

out. 'Begging to go back inside? Did you know that nearly ten thousand men are crammed into a jail built for... f... f ...,' she stuttered angrily, '...for less than a few thousand, human beings?' she said.

'Come, come Priscilla,' scolded her mother. 'Those so called human beings?' she paused and looked towards her husband, 'are our enemy and they must be treated as such. What has come over you, young lady?' she scolded.

Priscilla retorted angrily. 'This is insane! Sadistic! Inhumane!' she gathered her thoughts. 'The wanton cruelty,' said Priscilla. She paused briefly for breath. 'Captain, how can you treat humans like animals?' She shook with anger and took a huge breath before blurting out uncontrollably. '... cattle?'

Her father interrupted her. 'How would you have them treated? Sitting here at our table?' he said laughing and looking around for agreement.

'And, sharing Sir Thomas's fine wine?' continued Captain Shortland

There were loud guffaws of laughter from the men.

'Before we know it they will want to move into our homes,' mocked Sir Thomas.

'Who knows where it will end, eh, gentlemen?'

screeched the Captain.

'You call yourself gentlemen! How can you sit there and drink your wine, cognac and...,' she stopped to think pointing at the uneaten food on the table. 'Eat this food? Look at the waste. Those men are starving up there,' said Priscilla choking with emotion.

'Men!' roared her father.

'Animals! More like,' said Thomas Irwin finally feeling confident enough to join in.

'Even when we allow them to wash their filthy bodies, they choose not to do so. Disgusting vermin,' slurred the Captain before taking another slug of wine. 'They're alive with lice and creepers.'

'That's enough, Priscilla. It's most unladylike,' tutted her mother.

Captain Shortland shook his head.

'No, no, Dorien. Let her have her say,' he said drunkenly.

'That's as maybe, sir? But she is a lady and it is not befitting for a lady to talk in such a manner, sir,' said Dorien Irwin.

'Come, come, a toast for our host,' said Squire Irwin as he rose unsteadily from his seat and raised his glass.

'Sir Thomas,' he slurred before swallowing another glass of wine and falling back drunkenly into his chair.

ഇരു

🎗 Chapter seventeen 🎗

Squire Irwin and Thomas stood on the lawn shooting at makeshift targets nailed to the nearby trees while William Cole and Jeremiah Hatch, both chained at the ankle reloaded their rifles.

'Go and get me a drink will you, boy?' asked the Squire.

'Yessir,' replied William.

The guard released the manacles and William Cole limped awkwardly towards the house.

'Don't you think that you're a little too agreeable towards these men father? After all they are our enemy,' whispered Thomas Irwin.

Squire Irwin ignored his son. 'It's your shot, man!' he bellowed.

William Cole limped into the house and knocked gently

on the closed sitting room door.

'Come in,' shouted Dorien Irwin curtly.

William slowly opened the door and was taken aback at the moorland animal heads and stuffed birds that adorned every wall.

Dorien Irwin sat near the fire embroidering a silk handkerchief while Priscilla sat looking out of the window.

'Good afternoon, ma'am....' He turned to Priscilla, 'miss, I'm sorry to trouble you. The Squire has asked me to fetch him a cognac,' said William nervously.

Dorien barely looked up from her embroidery. 'Help yourself,' she said.

William didn't move and appeared reluctant to do so.

Priscilla smiled at him and pointed towards the ornate decanter. 'It's all right, I'll do it,' she said as she turned her wheel chair around. As she did so the shock was clearly visible on William Cole's face.

'It's all right. I said I'd do it, didn't I?' she snapped.

As she wheeled herself across the room, William's face suddenly changed.

'You look surprised,' said Priscilla.

'Well... yes... er... no,' stuttered William trying hard

to hide the shock. He shook his head slowly. 'I had no idea,' he said softly.

'Does it make a difference?' asked Priscilla.

She stopped in the centre of the room and waited. 'Be honest... I know it does. As soon as any man sees me like this they can't bear to even look me in the eye. They either take pity on me or never call again,' she said, her voice quivering with sadness.

She pulled a silk embroidered handkerchief from her sleeve and wiped her eyes. 'Who wants half a woman?' she asked.

William turned away.

'There you are...,' she said as she turned her head away. 'You're doing it,' she said sadly.

'No... I'm surprised that's all,' he said turning away from her to avoid her eyes. 'I really had no idea,' he said apologetically.

Priscilla poured the drinks and handed them to William.

'It was a riding accident. A fox spooked my horse,' she said as she remembered the moment. 'I broke my back,' she said as tears filled her dark green eyes.

'But... I saw you riding,' said William clearly

confused.

'Of course,' she said proudly. 'I'm not a total invalid. I can do most things but I quickly become weary. Father insists that I sit in this thing,' she said as she brought her hands down hard on the wooden wheels. 'He thinks he can control me like everyone else,' she said brusquely before turning and wheeling herself back to the window. 'That's enough about me,' she said.

She looked out across the moor and suddenly turned to him. 'Is it true about Thomas? Did he really kill someone?' she asked.

Her mother now looked up from her needlework. 'Priscilla, stop this nonsense!' she scolded.

William Cole nodded slowly, his face revealing the painful memory. 'Yes, miss.' He turned to Dorien Irwin and lowered his head. 'Ma'am... He shot my Captain...' he stopped, and remembered vividly that fateful morning. He coughed gently and continued in a sombre voice. '...Captain Coombes in cold blood.' He began to shake with rage. 'He didn't die immediately,' he said shaking his head wildly. 'It took best part of a week for him to die....' He hesitated. 'My Captain... chained like a common slave,' he said as he turned and looked out of the window at Thomas and the Squire. 'I'm sorry, miss, ma'am, your brother has a lot to answer for,' he said before turning to Priscilla and looking down at her wheelchair. 'And you, well... it really doesn't make any difference to me,' he said thoughtfully.

William walked across to her, placed the tray of drinks on her lap, smiled and pushed her towards the door, turning briefly to Dorien Irwin. 'Ma'am,' he said nodding slowly.

William pushed Priscilla into the garden and passed the Squire and Thomas their drinks. They ignored Priscilla; it was as though she wasn't there.

They finished their drinks and returned to their shooting.

'Come on! Quicker!' shouted an excited Squire Irwin.

William loaded two rifles while Jeremiah struggled to load the first.

Squire Irwin watched and realising that William was experienced he walked across to him. 'Can you shoot, boy?' he asked William tapping at the gun.

'I reckon I can, sir,' he replied

The Squire smiled widely. 'Show me,' he asked as he stepped back.

William took his gun, aimed at a pigeon as it flew out of the copse and fired. As the pigeon fell into the woods Priscilla smiled proudly.

'Excellent shot. What was the distance of that, man?' asked the Squire.

'A hundred yards or thereabouts, sir' replied William.

'Very impressive,' he nodded, 'yes, very,' he said stroking his beard. 'I'll have cook prepare that one for supper,' said the Squire as his face lit up and he whistled excitedly for his dogs to collect the kill.

Thomas Irwin looked away, cursed and kicked angrily at the lawn.

The Chief Revenue Officer accompanied by two additional Revenue men and three Marines rode up the long sweeping drive towards Captain Sleep's residence. They dismounted and passed their horses to one of the Marines and walked towards the imposing front doors.

The first Chief Revenue Officer knocked loudly on the door.

The doors slowly opened. 'May I help you, gentlemen?' asked the servant, taken aback by the visitors.

'We wish to address, Captain Sleep,' he asked

authoritatively.

'Shall I state you business, gentlemen? He asked.

'That won't be necessary,' said the second Revenue man.

The servant stepped aside. 'Gentlemen, please come in,' he said.

The servant walked through the impressive hall, followed by the Chief Revenue Officer and his men, knocked and entered the drawing room.

A large globe took pride of place in a room darkened by the carved hardwood furniture, dark oak timber floors and panelled walls much of which was covered with large paintings of ships and sea battles.

Captain Sleep sat in his large leather armchair reading and holding a glass of cognac while a long pipe smoked in the ash tray.

'You have callers, sir,' said the servant.

The Captain looked up and smiled, placed the glass and book on the table and stood to greet them.

'Captain Jonas Sleep?' asked the Revenue man.

'Yes, of course I am, sir,' replied Captain Sleep

The Chief Revenue Officer glanced suspiciously at the glass and nodded knowingly to his colleague.

'Captain Sleep, we have it on good authority that you are involved in defrauding His Majesty's Government.' He paused and licked his lips. 'Smuggling no less,' he said with a stern face.

'I beg your pardon, sir,' replied the Captain sternly.

The Revenue men looked at each other. 'Sir, we would like to search your premises,' said one of them.

The Captain was clearly angry. 'Now, just a moment,' he said looking around. 'On whose advice are you here?' he asked.

The Chief Revenue Officer stiffened. 'I'm afraid I can't divulge that, Captain,' he said.

Captain Sleep reached down, picked up his glass and emptied it with a large gulp. 'Please be my guest,' he said wiping his lips with a white handkerchief.

The two Revenue men left the room with one of the Marines while the third stood nervously at the door.

Captain Sleep refilled and lit his pipe and returned to his book as though nothing had happened.

In less than an hour the Revenue men re-entered the room accompanied by a Marine carrying a cask.

'Well Captain Sleep, sir.' The man turned and pointed at the cask before returning to face the Captain.

'This cask contains cognac and does <u>not</u> carry the Revenue stamp,' said the Chief Revenue Officer sternly.

Captain Sleep looked confused. 'What?' He turned to look at each his accusers before speaking. 'Damn you man, where did you find that?' he raged.

'In your stable, sir,' replied the second Revenue man in a restrained voice.

'You will need to accompany us to Plymouth, sir,' said the Chief Revenue Officer.

Captain Sleep looked at them transfixed as his face slowly drained of all colour.

The second Revenue man coughed nervously before speaking. 'Sir, you will need to accompany us, *now*,' he said firmly.

The Captain slowly rose from his chair. 'This is preposterous,' he said as he looked around the room. 'I've never heard anything so ridiculous in all my life.'

The servants acknowledged Captain Sleep in silence.

The Captain spoke clearly to his stunned servants as he was escorted past them. 'Tell Mrs Sleep, I will return before nightfall,' he said confidently.

The third Revenue man stopped and spoke to the servants. 'It is unlikely that the Captain will be back. We have indisputable success in matters of this nature... smuggling,' he said with a wide grin as he straightened his jacket. 'Generally... with hanging,' he said with a shrug. He shook his head and smiled at the servants, straightened his hat and pulled the front doors closed behind him.

The entourage, led by the Chief Revenue Officer followed by Captain Sleep and flanked by the Marines and Revenue men, left the Captain's estate and made its way in silence across the moor towards Plymouth.

As they neared Princetown, Thomas Irwin and Harold Thomson approached them, touched their hats, smiled broadly, kicked at their horses and raced on flaying their mounts unnecessarily.

Captain Sleep turned his head and followed them with his knowing eyes before gazing towards Plymouth, his uncertain future and what lay ahead.

Mara walked through the ill lit infirmary overflowing with sickly prisoners, her footsteps muffled by the incessant coughing and moaning.

Doctor MacGrath who was tending to a dying patient briefly looked up as she entered.

'Hello again, Mara, you're getting to be a regular

these days,' he said. 'Perhaps I should ask your father if you can help me?' he asked smiling at her.

She looked across to him and blushed. 'I already have,' she said softly.

'I wonder why?' he asked with a knowing smile.

Mara approached Peter Beck's bed. 'Hello Peter,' she said.

'Should you be here?' asked Peter trying to focus his eyes on the blurred outline.

'Don't worry about me,' she said firmly. 'How are you?'

Doctor MacGrath shouted across to her. 'He's doing very well, Mara.'

Peter tried to sit up but his heavily bandaged chest and leg prevented him from getting up.

'I've been better,' he sighed.

'Do you mind if I have a look?' she asked.

Peter nodded but as she slowly removed the blood encrusted bandages he screamed out in pain.

'I'm sorry Peter but I need to take these off,' she said as the smell of the poisoned flesh took her aback.

'I know,' he sighed.

Doctor MacGrath joined Mara and helped her to

remove the remainder of the bandages and when he saw the gangrenous wound and festering sores his screwed up his face confirmed his concern.

'We need to clean this up, and quick,' said Mara.

'We're doing the best we can... considering,' replied the Doctor.

Benjamin Beck pushed his way through the crowded market place and made his way towards Henrietta and Alex's stall.

'Hello,' said Benjamin nervously.

'How are you?' she replied straightening her dress and touching her hair nervously. 'Benjamin,' blushed Henrietta.

Alex giggled mischievously.

'I've been better,' he replied. 'How did you know my name?' he asked with a look of surprise.

'Yer friend told us,' she replied with a wide smile

Henrietta carefully chose some bread and a cake, wrapped them in a white cloth and placed them in his hands.

'This might help a little,' she said.

'Thanks,' he replied with an appreciative smile.

'Will I see you again, sir?' she asked.

'I'm not going anywhere... well not for a while,' he said, looking down at the food. 'I'll enjoy this, and yes... it will help.'

Mara made her way across the crowded square to Phinias and Giselle's stall, spoke briefly to Giselle, and bought some sphagnum moss, a wrap of white powder and a small bottle of coloured liquid.

Mara re-entered the infirmary and walked unnoticed past Doctor MacGrath who was attending to yet another dieing prisoner.

She walked across to Peter and lifted his head gently. 'Drink this, it will help you,' she said.

She poured a few drops of the coloured liquid between Peter's dry lips and carefully cleaned the leg wound before tapping the white powder onto it and binding the sphagnum moss tightly around it.

As Peter lost consciousness Mara knelt and kissed him on the cheek.

'Sleep well,' whispered Mara.

Benjamin Beck passed her on the way out, turned his head the other away and pushed past her.

Benjamin shook his brother. 'What's she doing here?' he gasped.

'Who? What?' asked a dazed Peter.

'She's the Agent's daughter. If he finds out,' he paused and looked nervously around. 'Well..., I don't dare think what he'll do to you.'

He looked down at his brother's leg. 'How does it feel?' he asked.

'Agony, absolute agony,' he said. 'Do you think they'll amputate?' he asked.

'I don't think so,' lied his brother.

Peter smiled at him and fell back to sleep.

Benjamin laid half the food he had been given by Henrietta on Peter's bed and left.

Joshua Amos lay on a makeshift bed which had been made up against the wall nearest to the fire.

'How do 'e feel today?' asked Giselle.

'A little better thank you,' replied Joshua Amos.

''E can stay 'ere as long as 'e wants. No one comes 'ere. But when they needs us they changes they're minds quick enough then,' she retorted.

'You be in the best place. From what I 'ear all's not well up at that prison. They're dieing like there's a plague,' she said thoughtfully.

Joshua looked into the fire and thought about his

fellow prisoners freezing back in the depot.

'Them knows you's 'ere and you be all right,' said Phinias.

He looked at Phinias and tried desperately to get out of the bed.

'What do you mean...? You've told Shortland I'm here?' he grunted, his face ashen with fear.

Giselle smiled and for the first time Joshua saw her real beauty.

'Us 'ould never do that,' said Phinias taken aback at the very suggestion.

'No, us 'ave told yer friends. They know you'm safe with us,' said Giselle proudly.

The Revenue man, hidden beneath the outcrop of trees gnarled and distorted by the fierce onshore winds, stood high on the cliff top and watched as the small craft made its way out to sea. He waited for Squire Irwin and the cart driven by Harold Thomson to make its way up the beach and onto the cliff track before he climbed onto his horse and, unnoticed, rode back towards Plymouth.

Graham Sclater

಄

ঙ৶ছ Chapter eighteen ঙ৶ছ

Rueben Beasly sat at the Agent's desk and two immaculate armed American Marines stood motionless beside him while Charles Blasden and Marshall Cunningham, as chosen representatives of the American prisoners-of-war, looked on.

Captain Shortland stood with his back to everyone and blew huge clouds of cigar smoke into the air as he looked out of the window.

'Captain, may I urge you on behalf of the American Government to show a little more... dare I say understanding towards my fellow countrymen,' said Rueben Beasly.

Captain Shortland turned and made no attempt to hide his anger.

'If your so called Government were more co-operative, then they would no longer be here,' he retorted.

'Please understand Captain, we are doing all we can to speed their release... but nevertheless it might be a few more weeks before we can do so.' He turned and addressed the prisoners. 'And then you will all be on your way home,' said Rueben Beasly with a forced smile.

He looked across at the Captain and waited for a reaction. When there was none he continued. 'Mind you, as far as you British are concerned it was just in time,' he grunted. 'You took a real thrashing at New Orleans in January,' he said laughing loudly his huge stomach rising and falling grotesquely.

'But the war was already over,' replied the confused Agent

'That's as maybe but no one knew it,' replied Rueben Beasly, with a hint of pride in his voice.

Captain Shortland frowned at him before lighting another cigar.

Marshall Cunningham stiffened and unable to hold back any longer spoke out.

'Who cares about the past, Mister Beasly, sir? You're not doing much to help us. Our men are dying quicker than they ever did at sea,' he shouted.

Rueben Beasly faked a laugh. 'Gentlemen, when I return to London I assure you I will do all I can to help your predicament.'

'Make it soon, Mister Beasly... make it soon,' said a dejected Charles Blasden wiping at his watery eyes.

Mara knelt beside Peter's bed and for the first time was able to smile. 'You look much better today,' she said excitedly. 'I've arranged to take you out onto the moor,' she said.

'How is that possible?' asked a confused Peter Beck

'You're in no fit state to run away are you, man?' said Doctor MacGrath.

'No, I don't believe I am,' replied Peter. 'Thank you, Doctor.' He forced a pained smile and turned to Mara. 'Mara, thank you,' he whispered and fell back exhausted.

Mara waited for a sunny day and that morning two guards carried Peter from the infirmary to the outer gate and helped him onto the cart. As he attempted to stand unaided, he stumbled but with the help of one of the guards he and Mara were finally ready to leave.

She drove the cart the short distance to Princetown through the square and down a narrow track between the Plume of Feathers and a cottage.

They travelled for almost a mile and passed the imposing Tor Royal on their left and continued in silence until they reached the open moorland.

Peter could see little more than shadows but he could hear the running water as it gushed over the large rocks and boulders.

'This is very kind of you, Mara,' he said taking in the bracing moorland air.

'I owe it to you, Peter. You saved my life,' she said.

'You don't have to do this,' he said reluctantly.

Mara sat in silence for a few minutes before she suddenly blurted out. 'You know you'll always have a limp, Peter,' she said sadly.

Peter smiled and slowly shook his head. 'I never ever thought I'd walk again,' he sighed turning to face her. 'So it really won't be a problem. Most of the cow hands back home have limps or some damage to their legs and arms,' he reassured her.

Mara smiled a relieved smile and took in the air before speaking.

'What's America really like?' she asked inquisitively.

'It's beautiful,' he reflected. 'Buffalos, thousands of 'em roam the plains. America is like nowhere else on earth,' he said pulling her closer to him. 'If we ever get to leave this place would you come back with me and Benjamin?' he asked.

'Me...? America?' shrieked a shocked Mara.

Her smiling face suddenly changed. 'I can't,' she said softly.

'Why?' asked Peter taken aback.

'What about my father? I can't just leave him,' she said thoughtfully.

'Don't you ever want a life of your own?' he asked brusquely.

'Well of course I do but I can't just leave him here. Surely, you of all people would understand it?' she replied harshly.

'It wasn't through choice that Benjamin and I found ourselves on that ship,' he retorted. 'We did it for our country. Mara, you must *understand* that?'

'I'm sorry, Peter. Of course I understand but I do have a choice and it's one I have already made. My father brought me up,' she reflected. 'He sacrificed his naval career for me and now you expect me to leave him after all he's done?'

'Done, what has he done?' he asked angrily.

She turned to face him. 'The sea he loves, for me,' she replied. 'Spending these last years in this God forsaken place so far from the sea, that's what he's done.' She climbed down from the cart and walked along the stream.

Peter felt strangely defenseless, but free. He tilted his head to one side and then the other as he listened to the skylarks as they sang high above him before diving headlong into the heather and their invisible nests.

Mara dragged her hands through the gravel before carefully choosing a pebble and drying it in her shawl.

Peter heard her footsteps on the gravel as she walked back to the carriage and climbed in. She pulled his arms around her, stroked his hair and kissed him on the lips for the first time.

'I'm sorry, Peter. I do understand your feelings but surely you must understand mine?'

'Of course I do,' he replied softly.

'This is a very special moment,' he said as he pulled her close to him and guided their faces in the direction of the sun. 'Why spoil it now?' he said.

She nodded her agreement but he couldn't see it.

She squeezed his hand firmly. 'I'm sorry, Peter. I

really am,' she said kissing him softly on the cheek.

He reached out and gently followed the contour of her lips with his index finger before speaking. 'How did you get a name like, Mara?' he asked.

'My father gave it to me. Mara is the Gaelic word for the sea,' she said. 'Very apt, don't you think since my father is a sea captain?'

'It is very unusual... and beautiful,' he sighed as he stroked her long dark hair.

'Peter, I have something for you,' she said as she took his hand and placed the smooth oval pebble in his palm. He rubbed it between his fingers before placing it in his pocket. 'It's beautiful; I'll keep it forever,' he said, 'my own piece of England.'

'I'm so glad you like it,' she said.

Mara smiled and looked out across the moor. 'It looks like another cold night,' she said pulling the blanket around Peter and her shawl around her shoulders.

'We should be getting you back to the infirmary, you must be exhausted,' she said.

'I am a little,' he replied. 'Thank you,' he said softly.

Graham Sclater

ഇൻൽ

ഇ Chapter nineteen ഇ

Sir Thomas Tyrwhitt entertained Captain Shortland, Squire and Thomas Irwin and Doctor MacGrath in his beautifully furnished library overlooking the open moor at the rear of Tor Royal. A number of wine bottles stood empty on the table and the air was thick with cigar smoke.

Unable to hold back any longer, Doctor MacGrath spoke out. 'You've got to do something to get them out of there. I've managed to save some by immunization... but not enough,' he said.

'That's as maybe but who's going to pay to send them back?' replied Captain Shortland ignoring the Doctor's concerns.

'We don't have the money and why should we pay for them, they declared war on us,' said Sir Thomas.

'Can't Beasly do anything to help?' asked the Doctor.

Captain Shortland stood and tapped his cigar ash into the blazing fire. 'He's about as much help as... well,' he stopped to think. 'I can't believe he's an American... and on their side,' he said, shaking is head in utter disbelief.

Sir Thomas shifted in his favourite chair near the fire. 'They'll just have to stay there until that dreadful man Beasly comes up with the money,' he said

'Here... here...,' agreed Thomas Irwin. 'As far as I'm concerned they can stay there and rot,' he said with a wide self congratulatory grin.

'Um... but for how long?' questioned the Doctor.

'As long as it takes, Doctor,' replied Thomas brusquely.

'But it might take forever,' said the Doctor his concerns clearly apparent.

'So what!' scoffed Squire Irwin.

Doctor MacGrath glared across at him. 'They've suffered enough and this ghastly war's over.' He stood to reinforce his anger and brought his clenched fists down onto the table. 'It's over, man! We've got no right to keep them locked up like....' He looked around the room and up at the stuffed trophies that adorned the wall above the wide fireplace. 'Like animals,' he shouted unable to hide his frustration.

The Squire nodded, looked across to his son Thomas and smirked. 'I've always thought the Doctor had a soft spot for the Yankees, eh Thomas?' he said.

There was as unexpected silence.

'Tell me, Captain,' asked Sir Thomas as he signalled to his servant who immediately rushed around the room pouring drinks. 'What do you think we should do with them? If we let them out surely they'll only die on the moor?' he asked.

'Yeah, perhaps even rape or murder our women,' scoffed Squire Irwin into his cognac.

Sir Thomas straightened his waistcoat. 'Exactly! That's why I'm thinking of arranging something... I thought that perhaps... a shooting competition to take their minds off the situation. The Prince of Wales will of course endorse it,' he said proudly.

Doctor MacGrath scowled.

'Shooting competition? What possible use is that?'

'Well... I think that it's a splendid idea?' said Squire Irwin as he took a huge drag on his cigar. 'We'll win of course,' he bragged.

Captain Shortland nodded in agreement.

'That Frenchie over at Tavistock, Monsieur Boulan, I'm sure he'll be only too pleased to represent his country,' he said laughing loudly.

'That's another poor sod. Is he still here in England?' asked the Doctor.

Thomas Irwin ignored him and spoke out. 'Monsieur Boulan? I saw him only last week, I'm sure he would be only too pleased to... to... extol the virtues of France,' he said with a loud mocking laugh.

Squire Irwin coughed loudly. 'And I, know just the man for the Yankees,' he said nodding slowly. 'William Cole is an excellent shot.'

'Not too good, I hope' scoffed Captain Shortland.

The Squire ignored his question and lit a cigar.

'Another glass, Squire Irwin, gentlemen?' asked Sir Thomas motioning to his servant once more.

Doctor MacGrath shook his head wildly and made towards the door.

'What is going on? Surely there are more important things to discuss than... a... a... a shooting competition?' gasped the Doctor lost for words.

Asha Adams rushed across the prison yard. 'They want someone who can shoot,' he shouted.

'Shoot what?' asked Ram Barley.

'Shoot who more likely,' answered Dylan Chipp.

'They've arranged a shooting competition. They want someone to represent us against the Frenchies and the guards,' explained Asha.

'There's only one choice as far as I'm concerned,' he paused and the prisoners stood open mouthed waiting for him to complete the sentence. 'And that's William... William Cole,' said Peter Beck.

The prisoners nodded in agreement.

'He shot Captain Sleep. Pity he didn't kill 'im,' mumbled Dylan Chipp.

He coughed, faked a smiled and looked around. 'Well, I think that all of you will want to put a wager on this one,' he said rubbing his hands wildly.

The daily market had finished and the market traders and merchants had already left. Any American prisoner able to stand waited in the yard and the militia and guards were grouped together laughing and already celebrating the anticipated outcome in what was an almost party atmosphere.

While Sergeant Greaves organized the makeshift thirty inch target at one end of the yard, William Cole,

Monsieur Richard Boulan, and Henry James, the chosen crack shot from the prison guards, nervously prepared their rifles fifty yards from it.

Captain Shortland sat in a large chair outside of his office, accompanied by an uninterested Mara.

He stood briefly and explained the rules. 'You will all take three shots at the target and whoever hits the inner target the greatest number of times will be deemed to be the winner. We have already drawn lots, and you will shoot in this order. Monsieur Boulan, Henry James and William Cole,' he said.

He lit a cigar and spoke through the thick smoke. 'Good luck gentlemen and don't forget, you are representing your respective countries,' he said.

He looked across at Henry James and smiled to him before sitting down.

Marshall Cunningham collected the last of the bets and handed the money to Dylan Chipp.

'No more bets, that's it. No more bets,' shouted a smiling and for once genuinely happy Dylan Chipp.

Sergeant Greaves signalled to the competitors and moved well away from the target while his assistant marked the firing position on the yard.

Richard Boulan held his hand high, threw a handful of straw into the air and watched it fall to the ground, nodded knowingly and adjusted his sights. He tucked the rifle in tight to his chin and fired. His first shot hit the inner area of the target. Clearly pleased with his effort, he grinned widely.

The prisoners jeered at him as he stepped back to reload.

Henry James took up his position, concentrated and aimed carefully at the target.

'Come on... show us what you can do,' shouted a voice deep in the crowd.

Henry James turned in the direction of the heckler grimaced and retook aim. His first shot also hit the inner circle of the target.

'That's not much better,' jeered the anonymous prisoner.

'Is that the best you can do?' shouted another.

'Yeah,' jeered the prisoners loudly and waving their arms around.

William Cole took his shot and hit the inner circle.

The American prisoners all sighed with relief.

Benjamin whispered in Peter's ear. 'We're all equal.'

Peter sighed heavily.

Richard Boulan stepped up to the mark and took his second shot and hit the outer circle.

The Americans jeered wildly and whistled at him.

Monsieur Boulan was clearly affected by the reaction although he tried to hide it by waving his arms in the air mocking victory before checking and reloading his rifle.

Henry James stepped up, took aim and fired.

He also hit the outer circle.

William Cole took aim and hit the outer circle and ignoring the misplaced congratulatory shouts turned to concentrate on preparing his rifle for his last and final shot.

Richard Boulan missed the target with his third and last shot. 'Merde!' he cursed and threw his rifle to the ground as the Americans jeered at him.

The guards and militia, sensing victory for their contestant, suddenly became very excited and cheered loudly as Henry James took aim and fired. He shook his head in utter disgust as Sergeant Greaves checked the position on his shot.

'Outer ring,' shouted the Sergeant.

The prisoners jeered at him as he walked off in

disgust not wanting to have his poor effort broadcast.

Benjamin leaned and whispered to Peter. 'William could win this, if he only hits the inner circle,' he said, his excitement rising.

There was total silence as William, nervously checked his rifle, aimed but then lowered it and checked it again.

'Come on William!' shouted a voice from the crowd.

'Yeah! Come on,' they shouted impatiently.

'Show the British bastards what you're made of,' shouted another.

He raised his rifle, fired and hit the centre of the target.

There was absolute pandemonium.

'We won! We won!' they shouted ecstatically.

Sergeant Greaves walked forward and rechecked the target. He looked back at Captain Shortland and reluctantly nodded.

There was absolute euphoria and the noise was deafening.

'Well done,' shouted Captain Shortland begrudgingly.

The prisoners rushed towards William and swamped him.

Captain Shortland drew heavily on his cigar. Although he wanted to continue, his attempts to speak were completely futile as he was drowned out by the Americans.

Henry James could not hide his anger, shaking his head in despair and embarrassment.

'All right… that's enough. Get back to your cells now,' boomed Sergeant Greaves fingering his whip.

'Good shootin' Will. You showed 'em good and proper,' shouted Asha Adams

The prisoners whistled, sang and talked excitedly about the afternoon while other groups played keno, a card game originating in China.

'That was some shootin' there, boy,' said Jeremiah Hatch.

'What with William and New Orleans we got 'em beat all 'round,' congratulated Asha Adams.

'Not before time,' said Marshall Cunningham.

Dylan Chipp smiled to himself as he paid out on the winning bets. He couldn't lose.

Hatred is the key

ഇൽ Chapter twenty ഇൽ

Captain Shortland paced his office and plugged angrily at his pipe, while Doctor MacGrath sat silently at his desk.

'The bastard! Beasly's got a lot to answer for....' He failed to finish the sentence instead he opened the door. 'Sergeant!' boomed Captain Shortland.

Sergeant Greaves rushed into the Agent's office.

Before he could speak Captain Shortland snapped at him. 'Go and get Mister Etherington,' ordered the Captain.

'Yessir!' replied the Sergeant,

The Sergeant returned a few minutes later with a flustered Marshall Etherington.

'We've got a problem, Mister Etherington,' he said sternly. Marshall Etherington tried to straighten his twisted misshapen frame as the Agent waved the letter in front of him.

'Your, Mister Beasly has stopped everyone's allowance,' continued Captain Shortland as he passed the letter to Doctor MacGrath.

'What's this all about, Captain Shortland, sir?' asked Ralph Etherington.

'You and your fellow Yankees will no longer get any money from your beloved America. Mister Beasly has advised us that since the war is over he no longer has the authority to continue to pay any allowances,' explained the Agent.

'He's done what?' exclaimed Marshall.

Sergeant Greaves stepped forward. 'You 'eard the Captain,' he said firmly.

Ralph looked at Captain Shortland his face clearly concerned and worried. 'I'll tell them, sir. But they won't like it,' he said.

'I don't see that they have any choice in the matter... do you?' asked the Agent.

'No, sir,' replied the prisoner. 'I don't.'

The bad news travelled fast and in less than an hour the yard was packed with angry prisoners-of-war.

A small group carried a full sized effigy of Rueben

Beasly across the yard and proceeded to put him on trial.

'Beasly! Beasly! Beasly!' chanted the angry prisoners as they continued to spill out into the yard.

His *effigy* pleaded guilty to neglect and for failing to repatriate the prisoners-of-war following the signing of the Treaty of Ghent and was paraded around the prison in front of an ever growing crowd of baying prisoners. As the tempers flared, his effigy was hung from a granite lintel and stoned by the prisoners with anything they could lay their hands on before being set on fire to riotous applause and jeers.

A group of Rough Alleys suddenly appeared from depths of the crowd and scrambled up the fence driving the sentries from their posts.

Pandemonium ensued as the remaining prisoners followed them and stood at the foot of the fence and tried to break it down.

Some of the inexperienced militiamen panicked and fired randomly into the air and as the alarm bells rang, they were immediately joined by reinforcements from the guardhouse while others soon arrived from Princetown.

Sergeant Greaves cracked his whip like a man possessed until another group of militiamen with their bayonets fixed, anxiously coerced the prisoners back towards the prison blocks.

Sergeant Greaves and the militiamen forced the prisoners into Number Three Block and slammed the door with a heavy thud.

'Captain Shortland has stopped all yer rations,' shouted Sergeant Greaves cockily.

The prisoners jeered angrily.

'Keep it down,' shouted the largest of the militiamen.

'And, you're confined to your block for twenty four hours!' shouted Sergeant Greaves.

The prisoners crowed loudly and as an act of defiance rattled and scraped their metal cups and dishes against the granite walls.

As darkness fell and the temperature once again dropped below freezing in the spring night, the moans and groans grew to an almost unbearable level.

'I'm starvin',' moaned Sylas.

'We're all starvin',' shouted Dylan Chipp.

'Shut up and get to sleep, we'll be out in the morning!' shouted Asha Adams.

Mara helped Peter to climb out of the cart and he used a makeshift walking stick to steady himself as she led him along the bank of the Blackbrook River. Thomas Irwin appeared from nowhere, jumped across the sheep leap and swept up beside them.

'Hello, Mara,' he said forcing a smile.

She chose to ignore him and they continued to walk.

Thomas followed closely and took his anger out on his horse by whipping him viciously.

'I don't understand you, Mara,' said Thomas faking yet another smile.

He trotted around in front of them, his horse visibly nervous.

'Why don't you spend your time with someone who can appreciate your beauty?' said Thomas looking across at Peter.

Mara and Peter continued to walk but Peter slipped and fell awkwardly cutting his hands on the jagged granite rocks as he fell awkwardly onto the gravel path.

Mara helped him to stand and carefully removed the gravel from the deep cuts in his bleeding hands.

'There..., see what I mean?' jibed Thomas.

'Peter, are you all right?' asked Mara.

Peter stood unsteadily trying to retain his balance and dignity.

'Yeah, I'm fine,' he said quietly.

He tightened his grip on the walking stick as his frustration and anger grew at his inability to protect himself.

Thomas dug his heels hard into the horses flank and continued to flay it unnecessarily with his whip.

Peter sensed the horse's fear and unnoticed by Thomas or Mara, contorted his mouth and let out a high pitched whistle.

The horse reared and Thomas was thrown from his mount and fell heavily onto the ground.

Mara shook her head at Thomas who lay moaning amongst the gorse.

She shrugged her shoulders and turned to Peter.

'Come on, Peter,' she said, as she guided him towards the cart.

'Damn you, Yankee,' seethed Thomas, as he rose gracelessly to his feet and looked out across the moorland for his mount.

The depot market square was crowded.

Thomas Irwin followed Mara at a distance and watched her every move.

She walked across to Peter and Marshall. She grasped

Peter's wrist and pushed a small parcel of food into his hand. He smiled and tucked it inside his shirt.

'Thank you,' he whispered.

On the other side of the yard the outgoing militiamen excitedly packed their equipment and prepared to leave.

'I shan't be sorry to get away from this place,' said a gaunt militiaman.

'Nor me,' answered another. 'The Somerset boys are welcome to it. Let's get as far away from 'ere as possible. The sooner the better,' he said.

The outgoing militia walked towards the gate and passed the rabble of the relief that was the Somerset militia. They tried to march in line but it wasn't possible.

'Good luck to ya. You'll need it,' shouted the gaunt militiaman

The outgoing militia marched out of the gate, whistling and much relieved.

The Somerset militia tried to take in their new surroundings but were overawed by the squalor and filth around them.

'Just look at this place. I reckon we're the prisoners. Not the bloody Yankees,' shouted one of them as the skies darkened and it started to rain heavily.

Sergeant Greaves stood proud and upright outside the Agent's office.

'Get to your quarters... and I want you all back 'ere in ten minutes. Look sharp now!' he boomed as he fingered his whip.

The militiamen broke ranks and ran blindly in the direction of the guard house.

Asha Adams ran from the yard and into Number Three Block. 'They've changed the militia. You should see 'em, a rabble to a man. Maybe it's a good time to get out of here,' he shouted excitedly.

No one listened to him.

Captain Shortland sat at his desk and alternated between drinking coffee and an almost empty whiskey bottle.

Doctor MacGrath sat opposite him drinking only coffee.

'Have you seen what they've sent me this time? Useless, no hopers, most of 'em have never used a gun in their life,' moaned Captain Shortland shaking his head. 'Um... I should be at sea doing what I do best. I'm not an agent, I'm a seaman. It's all I know,' he cursed.

He sipped at his coffee then his whiskey and lit

another cigar. 'When I shipped the convicts to New South Wales under Captain Phillips I never thought that I'd be doing anything like this. Look at this place, they're dying around us,' he said.

Doctor MacGrath looked up and spoke slowly. 'I know,' he said with a look of hopelessness. 'We've already lost more than fifteen hundred prisoners in this rotten place? But until this is over there's little we can do to change it.' He stood and looked out into the yard before he continued. 'Absolutely nothing,' he said. '...eighteen months in here seems like an eternity. How William Dykar stood it for so long I'll never know?' he sighed.

Before he could finish there was a loud knock at the door.

'Come in,' shouted the Captain.

Thomas Irwin entered flanked by Sergeant Greaves and a guard.

Finding it hard to catch a breath Thomas spewed forth. 'I saw him steal it... you need to put a stop to it or who knows what will happen out there,' he said pointing towards the yard.

Mara walked into the office and stood next to Doctor

MacGrath.

Thomas Irwin glanced across to Mara and continued.

'Captain, I saw a prisoner stealing food,' he said.

Captain Shortland rose unsteadily from his seat. 'What? Are you sure?' he asked.

'Captain Shortland, sir,' he took a deep breath. 'I saw him with my own eyes,' he said excitedly.

'Sergeant, whoever it is, arrest him and throw him in the *cachot* and,' he looked at the empty whiskey bottle on his desk and turned angrily. 'No rations for three days,' he boomed drunkenly.

Mara moved forward and made to speak. 'But...,' she gulped.

They all turned their attention to her.

Mara swallowed hard, looked across at Thomas and slowly shook her head. 'Um... nothing,' she murmured.

Thomas Irwin smirked and staring hard at Mara spoke out. 'Sergeant let me show you the vile criminal,' he said, before turning towards the still open door. 'Come!'

Thomas Irwin led the Sergeant and a group of guards out into the market square and pushed his way through the crowd. Without saying a word he pointed forcefully at Peter Beck his finger shaking with a perverse satisfaction and the widest imaginable grin across his smug face.

Three guards grabbed a stunned Peter who flayed out blindly in a pathetic attempt to ward off his unknown aggressors.

'Get off him,' screamed Benjamin as raced headlong across to his brother pushing his fellow prisoners aside. The guards were ready for him, and hit out violently with their rifles knocking Peter and Benjamin to the ground.

Thomas Irwin stood back and crossed his arms, posed arrogantly and watched as the guards dragged Peter from the mud and off towards the *cachot*.

Benjamin picked himself up and glared hard at Thomas. 'You bastard,' he seethed. He took a pace forward but three more guards were already walking towards him. 'You will pay!' He glared at him. 'Just wait and see.' He snarled as he wiped the blood from his nose and mouth with his sleeve before reluctantly turning away and kicking angrily at the mud and gravel.

The guards opened the heavy metal clad *cachot* door and threw Peter Beck inside.

He fell heavily and remained on the floor in the darkness. 'Help me! Anybody... please help me!' he cried.

From the darkness someone spoke out. 'You're wasting your time. Save your breath. You won't get out 'til they say so. You should know that by now,' said the voice.

Benjamin sat on the floor of Number Three Block and struggled to eat his meal.

'He must be starvin' in there,' he cursed.

'He can take it,' said Ram Barley

'I hope you're right,' replied Benjamin.

Graham Sclater

෨෨

ଈର Chapter twenty one ଈର

Joshua Amos watched Phinias and Giselle as they sat in silence staring at the circle of glowing candles.

'How dem people react to you's?' asked Joshua.

'React...? What do 'ee mean?' asked Phinias

''ow dey look ta you's?' replied Joshua.

'Do um?' replied Phinias tilting his head to one side.

'I dunno...,' she said. 'How do 'em *look* to us?' asked Giselle.

'You's must know you's... different?' said Joshua. 'Ain't you've sin it,' he said as he turned away from them.

'I mean,' Joshua paused, 'how they must look at da boat of you?' he said nervously.

Giselle moved from the table and sat beside him. 'Don't be tricked by what ya fink ya see. They all needs us...,' she said licking her lips. 'But they don't want others to know it,' she said with a knowing look.

Joshua was taken aback.

Giselle smiled at him. 'That surprises 'ee don't it?' she said. 'Us've bin on the moor since the *Beakers*, for more generations than any of us can ever remember,' she said proudly. 'Us used a live at Swincombe farm but when Tyrwhitt started buildin' Tor Royal us moved 'ere with mother. Us likes it 'ere, dun 'us Phinias?' she said.

'Yeah, us do,' replied Phinias as he poked at the logs. 'But 'tis further to walk to the depot,' he said thoughtfully.

Joshua nodded slowly and looked towards the fire his black face shining as it reflected the flames.

'Our mother brought Shortland's Mara into this world,' she said.

'She saved 'er life,' said Phinias proudly.

'Do 'ee know what, Joshua? He'd 'ave lost both of 'em if our mother hadn't been 'round to look out for 'im,' she paused and closed her eyes before suddenly opening them wide. 'Look at that,' she said pointing at the coloured bubbling liquid and coloured powders. 'We 'ave 'elped 'ee and it got 'ee better,' she said as she broke into a proud smile.

She looked pretty when she smiled thought Joshua.

''Ow's that there leg of yourn?' she asked.

Joshua smiled back at her. 'Dis fine,' he said rubbing his hand down his leg and stretching it. 'Dis fine fer sure,' he said as he subconsciously felt his ribs. 'Everyding's fine.'

'Answer me this question. Do ya believe that you'd still 'ave a leg if ya didn't cum to our door?' asked Phinias.

Giselle answered for him. ''Course not. You'd be like all the others, on sticks... no good to man nor beast,' she said knowingly as she winked at him.

'We live in this cottage on Captain Sleep's estate and we help 'im when 'is animals is sick and sometimes when his servants am taken bad,' she said reflecting.

She reached across to the glass tank, removed the biggest toad, stroked it and then tickled its fat throat. The toad croaked loudly as though he was talking to her.

'We mean no 'arm to anybody. Is that right Phinias?' she asked.

'Das right,' he said. 'Nobody,' he replied turning to Joshua and smiling.

'Do 'ee wanna 'old 'im,' she asked as she offered the toad to Joshua.

He shook his head. 'No... I don't,' he said emphatically.

Giselle laughed loudly and kissed the toad before placing it back in the tank.

'I wanna show 'e somethin' else,' she said rising from the table.

The metal clad door opened and Peter Beck stumbled out of the cachot.

Benjamin helped him up but it was obvious that once again he was very sick.

'Give me a hand will yer! I need to get him to the infirmary,' shouted Benjamin.

The nearest guard pointed at Ralph Etherington. 'You! Give 'im an 'and and I want you back in five minutes or you'll find yourself in there,' he roared pointing towards the *cachot*.

Benjamin and Ralph carried Peter into the ward. 'Help me! Somebody help me!' pleaded Benjamin.

Doctor MacGrath looked up from his patient and attracted the attention of an orderly.

'Put him over there and get me some blankets...

quickly,' he ordered.

George MacGrath finished with his patient and crossed to look at Peter, covered him with the new blankets and wiped his forehead.

'Leave him here. I'll do what I can,' said the Doctor shaking his head slowly. 'I don't know how much more this one can take,' he said quietly.

Mara stood in the shadows and held back the tears and waited for Benjamin and Ralph to leave.

She stepped nervously forward, leaned over Peter and wiped his forehead.

'Is it right? The war's over,' asked a delirious Peter Beck.

'Yes, it is,' replied Mara.

'I thought I'd dreamed it,' said Peter.

'It is over and you'll be able to go home when Beasly makes the arrangements,' she said as she caringly washed his face.

'You're sad about that aren't you?' he asked.

Mara stopped and stroked his forehead pushing his long hair from his eyes. 'I'm happy for you but I'm sad for myself. You'll soon be going back to your family in America and I'll be left here in this terrible place,' she said sadly.

'Mara, you know you can come with me if it's what you really want,' he said.

'I know,' she replied. She turned her head away and dabbed at the tears with her handkerchief.

The night sentries stood on the walls oblivious to the lone figure who had climbed onto the roof of Number Three Block.

It was a grey wet morning but the prisoners stood around in the rain and whispered excitedly to each other.

Captain Shortland stood outside his office with Sergeant Greaves and when he noticed the American flag he took a huge breath of anger before speaking.

'Who is responsible for this?' he raged.

There was a lengthy silence.

Several pigeons flew across the yard. The prisoners looked up at them and silently envied the freedom they enjoyed.

'Find him, Sergeant Greaves! I'll have him flogged!' screamed the Captain. He paused and spat venomously, between his cigar stained teeth, in the direction of the prisoners. 'Come forward now or you will all face ten days in the *cachot!*' he raged.

No one moved.

The tension continued to build for several minutes until Miles Longman nervously shuffled forward.

Captain Shortland smiled and slowly licked his lips.

Sergeant Greaves fingered his bullwhip in anticipation.

Ram Barley stepped forward, followed by Thomas Johnson, then Marshall Etherington and slowly everyone else followed until the yard was full.

Captain Shortland pointed at the American flag flying above Number Three Block.

'Sergeant Greaves... get that thing down... now!' he bellowed

'Yessir!' snapped the Sergeant.

While Sergeant Greaves motioned to two guards to climb onto the roof and remove the flag the prisoners erupted into raucous laughter, clapping, jeering and celebratory handshakes.

The market traders began to enter the square and ignorant of the American flag proceeded to set up their stalls before stopping to cheer with the prisoners.

Captain Shortland suddenly lost his temper. 'Get 'em out of here! You heard what I said!' he snarled.

He looked around, his fingers twitching with anger.

'No! There will be <u>no</u> market today!' he screamed.

The traders looked at him bewildered and confused.

'Captain, we'm come all the way from Plymouth,' shouted Martha. 'Me fish'll go rottin',' she pleaded.

Captain Shortland stared at her for a while, took a huge drag on his cigar and exhaled the thick smoke, obscuring his face. He waited for it to clear before giving her a nefarious glance. 'It's already rotten,' he drawled. 'Away with you... all of ya... now!' he boomed.

Without another word the traders dismantled their stalls, packed their goods and left.

As the prisoners scuffled with the militiamen, several of them were beaten by the rifle butts and spiked with the bayonets until order was finally resumed.

The prisoners were manhandled into Number Three Block and the door at one end of the block was closed and locked. They stood and waited impatiently for their food and the closing of the second door. It didn't happen and the guards remained in position, motionless.

'Why don't you bastards just let us go home?' shouted Jeremiah Hatch.

'Can't you accept the bloody war's over?' goaded

Dylan Chipp.

'I'll find a way and while I'm at it I'm gonna kill that bastard Sergeant,' screamed Benjamin Beck, his voice cracking with sheer anger.

'Yeah! There's no way they're keeping me in this rat infested hole any longer,' shouted Robert Stapley.

The block erupted with screams, taunts and shouts of agreement.

Asha Adams suddenly lost it and rushed at the guard standing nearest to the open door but was immediately knocked down by a second guard.

Many of the other inmates joined in and waged a violent attack on the guards until Sergeant Greaves and reinforcements arrived and forced the prisoners back inside.

'You're a dead man when we get out of here!' screamed Thomas Johnson

The Sergeant cracked his whip defiantly. 'Shut up or you'll get the same as 'im,' he snarled, pointing at Asha Adams who lay moaning and bleeding on the granite floor.

The injured guards were carried away and Sergeant Greaves locked the door.

Reluctantly some of the prisoners now turned their attention to Asha Adams.

'If you really want to break out, we've got to plan it or we'll all end up in the *cachot*,' said Benjamin Beck.

'Or dead,' said Thomas Johnson.

'Yeah, the bastards will love that. Any excuse to kill us,' shouted Marshall Cunningham out of the darkness.

Asha Adams was helped to his feet, wiped the blood from his face and checked his bruised ribs as he struggled to speak. 'Do they need an excuse to do anything?' he asked. 'No, they can do what the fuck they want,' he moaned.

Dylan Chipp stepped forward. 'I'm starving. Thanks to you we'll get nothing tonight,' he said.

Asha Adams struggled to speak through his bleeding mouth. 'It wasn't that many months ago when you refused to eat anythin' in here,' he said trying to force a pained smile.

'Yeah, that's right, ma Lord,' mimicked Marshall Cunningham.

Hatred is the key

೮೦೧೩

෨෨ Chapter twenty two ෨෨

While Captain Shortland sat behind his desk and smoked his long pipe, Sir Thomas Tyrwhitt stood near the window smoking a large cigar and watching the prisoners playing football.

Robert Stapley deliberately kicked the ball over the wall and seconds later it was thrown back by a guard.

'Captain, the Prince of Wales has raised the matter with the American Ambassador and there is nothing that he or America can do,' said Sir Thomas.

Captain Shortland fingers twitched with anger.

'The Ambassador has assured the Prince of Wales that he will keep Beasly advised and when I receive instructions you will be the first to know...,' said Sir Thomas taking a long drag on his cigar. 'But until then....' He stood and thought before he continued. 'They remain your guests,' he teased. 'Please treat them well, Captain,' he said. 'Treat them well.' He tapped the ash from his cigar and continued. '...after all they are our reluctant guests.'

Sir Thomas left Captain Shortland's office and escorted by Sergeant Greaves walked toward the gate and his waiting carriage which took him the short distance to the church and Emily's christening.

Benjamin Beck, Robert Stapley, Asha Adams, Miles Longman and Marshall Cunningham and Charles Blasden and several other prisoners played football.

Benjamin saw Peter with Sylas and stopped playing and led him across the yard.

Robert deliberately kicked the ball high over the wall.

The prisoners waited for a few minutes, but when it is not returned Charles Blasden walked towards the wall.

Robert Stapley kicked a second ball hard and sent it high over everyone's head and into the outer yard. He and his fellow players waited patiently and peered up into the bright late afternoon sun. But when the ball failed to be returned he and Charles made their way to the small cracks in the pointing between the rough hewn granite blocks that they had all subconsciously picked at in the hours and months of boredom.

Charles screwed his face and peered through the thick wall at the nearest guard.

'Come on, get it back over here then,' he screamed.

The guard chose to ignore him and continued to talk to the sentry on the wall high above him.

'Come on you bastard, you heard me... kick it back,' shouted Robert. He waited impatiently, his body shaking with a mixture of anger and frustration.

The guard gave a shrug of indifference, smirked and walked off in the direction of the guardroom.

Robert finally lost control. 'If you don't, we'll come and get it,' he shouted.

His threat fell on deaf ears and swearing through his steaming breath he knelt on the wet stony uneven ground, oblivious to the pain as the jagged pieces of granite cut deep into his bare knees. He dug wildly with his bare hands until the nails ripped from his bleeding fingers.

His obsession soon spread and within a few short minutes Charles, Sylas and several other prisoners joined him to dig feverishly at the base of the wall.

As they ripped at the wall the smaller pieces of granite fell away and they threw them at the sentries.

The nearest sentry reacted by panicking and thrusting his rifle towards them. 'They're trying to escape!' he screamed.

Immediately the deafening, ear-splitting barrage of drums, calling the Marines to arms reverberated off the stone buildings back across the yard and onto the open moor.

The prisoners, already in their cell blocks, shocked and taken by surprise at the noise, rushed out of the buildings, spilling excitedly into the yard.

'What the hell's goin' on?' questioned Ram Barley.

'We're getting outta here,' replied Charles without taking his eyes off of the ever-growing hole at the base of the wall.

As the numbers started to swell the Rough Alleys rushed forward chanting their watchword, 'Keno! Keno! Keno!'

Without wasting any more time they began to hack at the gates impatiently with makeshift tools, pieces of wood and metal ripped out of the buildings. Their efforts were futile but other prisoners soon joined them and the gates gave way under the sheer weight of numbers and they spilled triumphant into the next yard.

Captain Shortland and Doctor MacGrath accompanied by Sergeant Greaves appeared at the door of the Agent's office and waited while more guards rushed out to join them on the opposite side of the prison yard.

Captain Shortland looked towards the nervous sentry on the wall. 'What's going on, man?' he screamed.

'Sir, they're trying to break out!' replied the terrified guard.

By now nearly four thousand American prisoners had gathered excitedly in the yard while a never ending stream of captives gushed out to join them from the other Blocks. Captain Shortland could feel the tension building between the prisoners, the ill trained militia and his guards. 'Get back to your cells...,' he screamed. He lowered his head and dug his boot hard into the mud before slowly raising his head and glaring at them. 'Now!' he roared.

For a split second everyone stopped and there was total silence as they stood staring at him defiantly.

Some of the prisoners kicked at the ground while others fidgeted nervously.

'We don't want any trouble; you'll all be going home

soon,' said Doctor MacGrath as he stuttered nervously and tried desperately to reassure the prisoners.

At first it appeared to have the desired effect until a lone voice shouted out of the crowd. 'Break outta here, come on!' he shouted.

'The war's over,' shouted another. It was the only encouragement they needed as they slowly pushed forward.

'Yeah,' jeered the angry crowd. 'Break out! Break out! Break out!' they chanted.

'Keno! Keno! Keno!' shouted the Rough Alleys as they collectively thrust their clenched fists high in the air.

Doctor MacGrath stepped forward. 'You all know you'll be going home soon,' he said, trying desperately to defuse the situation.

The prisoners pushed and shoved the line of guards and militia towards Captain Shortland while others systematically pelted their captors with stones and larger rocks, many hitting their targets, inflicting cuts and deep bloody lacerations.

'Listen to me, will yer,' screamed Doctor MacGrath his voice cracking with nerves and emotion. 'Go back to your blocks, ple... ease,' he begged.

They chose to ignore him instead raising their fists to further antagonise Captain Shortland, Sergeant Greaves and the guards.

As more and more lethal makeshift projectiles found their targets the mob grew in confidence, raising their fists, jeering and taunting their captors.

'Break out! Break out! Break out!' they continued to chant.

The Somerset militiamen gripped their rifles, fingered their triggers and looked nervously around for orders.

Captain Shortland ordered the bugler to sound the alarm and immediately the drummers 'beat to arms.' The noise was deafening as the thunderous sound of the drums reverberated once again from the granite buildings and across the prison yard.

In sheer desperation Captain Shortland, gave his command. 'Come to the present!' he ordered.

While the dazed guards and militiamen tried to level their rifles to waist height the frenzied prisoners rushed defiantly forward and wrestled fiercely with them rendering many of their long time aggressors defenceless.

Captain Shortland gave his next command. 'Fire!' he

screamed.

The guards and militiamen fired their rifles harmlessly into the air while the dazed prisoners stood and looked on. The militiamen and guards used the valuable time to reload, frantically ramming their rods down the barrels.

'They're firing blanks!' screeched William Cole, in a combination of excitement and disbelief.

The prisoners now gained confidence and slowly pushed forward building momentum until they broke into a run and rushed the remaining militia.

High on the wall, the strategically positioned sentries waited for their instructions and prepared to fire.

Throughout the bedlam and chaos Henry James held his rifle tight to his chin and continued to maintain William Cole in his sights.

Captain Shortland knew only too well that the situation was hopelessly out of control and while he considered all possible options a voice in the crowd made the decision for him.

'Fire!' someone screamed.

As soon as the lone powerful word rang out volleys of carefully targeted shots thundered down from the prison walls.

Henry James was the first to shoot, he aimed at William Cole squeezed the trigger and fired.

William spun around and fell to the ground, dead. Henry's shot hitting William Cole in the centre of his forehead.

Henry James tilted his head proudly back. 'Got you, you bastard,' he said as he gave a satisfied grin before he frantically reloaded.

The prisoners continued to pelt the guards with stones as they rushed forward.

The guards on the wall fired an arc of shots into the massed prisoners and, caught in the crossfire many of them fell heavily, still screaming as they hit the ground.

Others died silently without uttering another word.

Thomas Johnson pulled a knife from his boot and ran at Miles Longman. Miles was about to throw a large rock in the direction of the militiamen and was caught totally unawares by the vicious attack from behind. They both fell to the ground and wrestled, rolling in the mud amongst the dead and dieing Americans and injured militiamen. Miles, the much stronger of the two men, grabbed Thomas's throat and his strong thick fingers dug into the soft flesh beneath his chin piercing his windpipe.

He tore the knife from Thomas and stabbed him in the chest several times before letting his lifeless body drop to the ground.

Sergeant Greaves strode forward, pulled back his bullwhip, and aiming at Miles, swung it with lethal accuracy. It wrapped around the thick neck of black slave and tightened like a boa constrictor. Although Miles struggled to pull it loose, it grew tighter and tighter until he fell heavily to the ground. He had no chance, the well-worn leather choking the very life out of him.

As Sergeant Greaves walked towards the dead Negro to retrieve his whip, Ram Barley appeared from nowhere, grabbed it and wrestled the Sergeant to the ground as they fought for their very lives.

The light from the log fire along with the candlelight cast strange dancing shadows around the walls of the dimly lit cottage. Phinias sat at the table filling small green and brown phials with different coloured liquids, while Giselle sat in front of the fire with Joshua. Unnoticed, she pulled a piece of cord around the neck of an effigy of Sergeant Greaves.

Ram Barley pulled the bull whip around the bruised neck

of Sergeant Greaves and choked the life out of him.

The guards on the wall fired indiscriminately into the fighting crowd while the Americans continued to fight viciously with the militia and guards that quickly surrounded them.

While everyone else tried to escape from the yard Peter Beck, unable to see what was going on and an easy target for even the poorest shot gyrated wildly on the spot and shook his head violently. 'Help me! Help me! Benjamin, help me!' he repeated before he let out a high pitched blood curdling scream.

Benjamin rushed towards his brother grabbed him and tried to pull him to the ground but as he did so he drew even more attention to them and the sentries high on the inner wall turned in their direction and fired volley after volley at them.

Benjamin fell to the ground.

Peter reeled and followed him and lay motionless across his brother's body.

Ram Barley raced across the yard and as he hid behind Charles Blasden, a shot passed through his armless sleeve and into the Ram's naked chest.

As the uninjured prisoners raced back towards their

cell blocks, they were chased by the armed militiamen and guards who emitted bloodcurdling screams as they lunged out at them aggressively with their fixed bayonets.

Desperate to escape the threatening militia and guards the prisoners rushed into the prison blocks, screaming as the long period of hate finally erupted and each side released its anger.

The militiamen slashed and jabbed their bayonets randomly at the unarmed prisoners, who attempted to escape by swinging the hammocks haphazardly at their aggressors, but could find nowhere to hide.

A prisoner wounded by the gunfire knelt and begged for mercy but without a word from his attackers he was repeatedly bayoneted to death in cold blood.

The remaining prisoners fought back and attacked the guards and militia with anything they could lay their hands on throwing their meagre belongings at them, metal cups, plates, blankets before cutting down their hammocks and throwing them.

Graham Sclater

෨◌ଓ

∞∞ **Chapter twenty three** ∞∞

Emily had been christened on her first birthday at a private service attended by Mara Shortland, Captain and Judith Sleep, Isaac and Rachel Hartman and their guest of honour, Sir Thomas Tyrwhitt, before travelling to celebrate at the Hartman residence.

'Happy birthday, little one,' said Captain Sleep.

'This is a little something for Emily,' said Judith Sleep.

Judith passed a silver bracelet to Rachel who placed it on Emily's tiny wrist.

'Who's a lucky girl? It's lovely, isn't it Emily,' cooed her mother.

'Today... the 6th April, was also my mother's birthday,' said Mara sadly.

Judith held Emily while Mara lit the single candle on the birthday cake and they all cheered and clapped enthusiastically.

'Blow, Emily,' said Rachel.

While Isaac helped Emily to blow out the candle Sir Thomas poured the sherry.

Janice Hephzibah, a teenage servant, rushed into the room followed by Joe, the stable boy.

'Sir, ma'am, there's trouble... trouble at the depot!' stuttered Janice trying desperately to catch her breath.

'There's... mayhem! Mayhem!' interrupted Joe.

Emily mumbled innocently as Rachel took her from Isaac and held her close to her breast.

'What did you say...?' asked Isaac Hartman not realising that Rachel had taken Emily from him.

'Janice... Joe... what are you talking about?' asked Mara.

Joe moved into the centre of the room, his eyes red and swollen, and tried to speak slowly. 'At the depot, sir... ma'am,' he sobbed uncontrollably. 'The guards fired on them Yankees. They're trying to break out!' he exclaimed.

'I don't believe it, Joe. Tell me again and this time... slowly,' coaxed Captain Sleep.

Joe repeated what he had already said to a transfixed audience.

The colour suddenly drained from their faces.

'I wondered when...,' muttered Sir Thomas failing to finish his sentence and placing the silver tray and celebratory drinks on the side board.

Isaac Hartman walked to the door. 'Come Captain!' he sighed. 'Such a sad day for your birthday, Emily,' he said looking across tearfully at his baby daughter and Rachel.

'I'm coming with you,' said Mara, as she joined him at the door.

Beneath the deep threatening rain clouds Captain Sleep, Isaac Hartman, Mara and Sir Thomas Tyrwhitt made the short distance in his carriage across the moor and into Princetown.

As the carriage approached the prison they could see a crowd had already gathered and nearest to the entrance stood Thomas Irwin.

They climbed out of the carriage and rushed towards the prison gates and the now smirking Thomas. He sidled up to Captain Sleep and spoke slowly savouring every word. 'I hope you feel proud of your achievement..., Captain,' he said. 'You brought them all here to die, their contempt for you kept them alive.' He continued to goad Captain Sleep, 'their hatred for you gave them the key, sir.'

His face suddenly became horrifically distorted as he unleashed the sickening hate. Thomas stood glaring hard at Captain Sleep, his fingers shaking uncontrollably.

Mara rushed towards Thomas and blindly hit out at him. 'You bastard!' she screamed.

'Don't waste your time on him, ma'am. He's really not worth it,' boomed Isaac Hartman.

Captain Sleep walked up to him stopping a few inches short of his smug face.

'Sir, is it beyond you to show some compassion?' He could feel the rage building up inside him. 'Damn you, man!' he snarled and stormed off.

It began to rain heavily, as the group walked into the prison to find Captain Shortland standing in the centre of the yard his face cupped in his bloody hands and repeating the same phrase over and over. 'Somerset militia, who gave the order? Somerset militia, who gave the order? Somerset militia, who gave the order?' he mumbled incoherently.

When the group took in the carnage around them they shook their heads at the sheer horror.

'No!' screamed Mara, her voice reverberating around the now silent yard.

She pushed past her father and ran towards the piles of contorted lifeless bodies passing from one group to the other, searching desperately amongst the dead and wounded.

Sir Thomas Tyrwhitt, Captain Sleep and Isaac stood and looked on in disbelief.

'The Prince Regent will be outraged by this,' muttered Sir Thomas.

Captain Sleep nodded his silent agreement.

Mara reached Peter and Benjamin.

They lay motionless against the palisade fence amongst several dying and dead blood drenched prisoners.

She bent down and stared blindly at them before kneeling in the crimson mud.

Her whole body shook with horror as she cried and moaned powerlessly as involuntary shudders wracked her body and she bit hard into her knuckles.

Captain Shortland lowered his hands to reveal his traumatised and ashen face and continued to stare blankly ahead.

Benjamin, in obvious pain, cried out. Peter attempted to sit up but unable to do so Mara cradled him in her arms and made a feeble attempt to staunch the blood streaming down his forehead and into his eyes.

He tried to reach across to his brother, sobbed and slumped against Mara.

'What have they done to us?' mumbled a confused Peter before losing consciousness.

'He'll be all right, Benjamin' sobbed Mara shaking with emotion. 'You're both going to be fine,' she said reassuringly.

'No... he can't die! We're going home,' screamed Benjamin.

'I'm sorry Benjamin... I really am so very sorry... we've got to get you both to the infirmary,' she said in desperation.

She stood and shouted at Doctor MacGrath and the orderlies who were tending to wounded prisoners on the other side of the yard. 'Doctor, quickly!' she screamed.

He briefly looked up to her and continued to treat the wounded guard.

'Doctor MacGrath, over here!' she screamed, but this time she waved her arms wildly.

The Doctor left the wounded guard with his orderlies and made his way to her ignoring other wounded prisoners, guards and militia as he passed.

He carefully parted the blood soaked hair on Peter's head, checked the gaping hole in his skull and pushed a towel tightly around his head to stem the bleeding before turning his attention to his slashed face and placing another towel over the wound.

He now turned his attention Benjamin.

'Don't worry about me... I'll be fine... just take care of Peter will you, Doctor?' gasped Benjamin.

Doctor MacGrath, with a concerned look on his face, nodded and stood up. He motioned to his orderlies to assist him.

They ran across the yard and lifted Benjamin onto the first stretcher. Peter began to moan, gradually regained consciousness and tried to stand.

'Don't attempt to get up, Peter, we'll take care of you,' said the Doctor.

The militiamen moved closer and pointed their bayonets menacingly at the brothers thrusting them ever nearer as they grew in confidence.

Doctor MacGrath suddenly lost his temper. 'Can't you

two fools see that these poor men are going nowhere!' he screamed. 'Get away from me! Get out of my sight!'

They looked at each other, reluctantly lowered their rifles and skulked off towards the guard house.

Mara continued to stroke Peter's bloody face and pressed her other hand firmly on his serious head wound.

'Yes, listen to Doctor MacGrath, Peter. He knows best,' sobbed Mara uncontrollably.

Benjamin began to convulse violently and kick out.

The Doctor motioned to the orderlies to lower the stretcher to the ground and he knelt beside him and tried desperately to help him.

Benjamin coughed heavily and suddenly stopped moving.

Doctor MacGrath turned and looked up at Mara. His strained face was slowly transformed into a look she had seen much too often since frequenting the infirmary; the look of imminent death.

Her whole body quivered with shock as Doctor MacGrath slowly shook his head, reached down and sensitively covered Benjamin's face with the bloodstained blanket.

Peter pushed himself up and rested on his elbow but fell back onto the mud before crawling over to Benjamin and cradling him in his bloody hands.

'Why him!' he screamed. 'My brother had so much to live for... it's this place!'

He stopped suddenly and a tormented high pitched squeal emanated from his throat. 'Your father...,' he looked around blindly. 'He did this, didn't he?' he sobbed.

Mara looked at Peter as though he could see her. 'I'm so sorry,' she mouthed remorsefully.

She tore at her long wet hair and shook her head in despair.

'I don't know,' she replied wiping her eyes. 'I just don't know...,' she sobbed violently. 'He's not a bad man,' she looked at her father who remained transfixed in the yard. 'He's not!' she screamed. 'He's not!'

Captain Shortland turned and walked slowly towards his office, his shoulders hunched and head bent forward.

A broken man.

The remaining militia and guards stood nervously in the rain. Motionless, they held their ground, their rifles and bayonets pointing defiantly in front of them.

Sir Thomas Tyrwhitt, Captain Sleep and Isaac Hartmann stood and continued to look on in disbelief at the utter carnage. They watched in silence as Doctor MacGrath carefully inspected every prisoner in the yard for any sign of life and identifying them to the orderlies before he walked nervously towards Number Three Block.

'It's over now... it's over,' he repeated reassuringly.

The Doctor entered the dark and threatening prison block, the only light came from the lantern held by his assistant. He walked in the direction of the moans and groans. Other prisoners, waited in the shadows menacingly, while others hid and peered nervously in his direction.

'It's over now... it's over,' he continued to repeat reassuringly.

Benjamin Beck, Thomas Johnson, Miles Longman, Sergeant Greaves and many more were lifted from the blood stained mud and carried towards the mortuary.

Dylan Chipp sat up slowly and closely examined the blood covered suit. 'Damn!' he moaned

He stood, checked his pockets and discovered that the inner lining had been sliced through. 'My money's gone!'

he shouted. 'Who stole my money?' he raged. 'I've been robbed!'

No one cared.

Charles Blasden got up and poked his finger through the hole in the sleeve of his jacket. 'Thank God, I didn't have an arm in that,' he laughed uncertainly, realising that he had survived yet again.

Henrietta and Alex stood soaked to the skin and waited in the cold clear night as the last of the rain clouds were blown across the moonlit sky.

The gates opened and when they saw Captain Sleep and Isaac, the sisters ran towards them.

'Is it true? Tell me it's not, please tell me,' asked a breathless Henrietta

'I'm afraid it is,' replied Captain Sleep softly.

'Is Benjamin all right?' asked Henrietta anxiously.

Captain Sleep, his face tired and drawn, stooped down to her. 'I don't know… it's much too early but there are many injured and unfortunately many dead,' he said sadly.

Isaac put his arm around her shoulder and pulled her into his chest. 'Come back tomorrow. That's best,' said Isaac, shaking his head uncontrollably.

'But...,' pleaded Henrietta as tears poured down her innocent cheeks.

Isaac looked at her, took a handkerchief from his jacket pocket and gently wiped her tears. 'Tomorrow,' he said softly as he tried to hide his tears. 'Come back tomorrow.'

Alex tried to console her broken hearted sister as they made their long journey back across the moor to their farm.

Captain Shortland sat at his desk in near darkness with an almost empty bottle of cognac within arms reach. He held a glass awkwardly in his hand and sat staring at the wall.

Mara entered the office. 'What have you done?' she asked her voice breaking as she sobbed wildly.

Her father looked at her vacantly. 'I don't know what happened.... One minute they were jeering and the next... the shots....' He covered his face and took a deep juddering breath. 'It was a massacre, a cold blooded massacre. I tried to tell them but no one listened,' he said his voice quivering with emotion.

The next morning there was an eerie silence across the depot yard. The spring sun shone as the armed guards stood uneasily around the perimeter walls their fingers twitching nervously on the triggers of their rifles.

The uninjured prisoners moved solemnly around the reduced paved area of the yard in a state of shock and disbelief and paid no attention to the groups of militia and guards who worked in silence clearing the blood stained mud, loading it into carts and replacing it with clean granite chippings.

The groans and moans of the dieing and wounded prisoners resonated throughout the infirmary as an exhausted Doctor MacGrath made his way slowly through the packed building checking each of his patients as he passed. He stopped periodically to check the severely wounded and covered their faces as they died.

Mara sat beside the heavily bandaged Peter.

She held his hand and prayed.

'Miss Shortland, you should get some sleep,' pleaded the Doctor.

'No, Doctor MacGrath, I'm not leaving Peter this time,' she said defiantly.

Unnoticed by anyone, Peter squeezed the pebble in his hand.

Captain Shortland entered the deserted cemetery and shuffled towards his wife's grave. He slipped onto his knees and cried violently.

'What have I done?' he screamed.

He shook his head erratically and sobbed.

He reached out blindly, tilted his head to one side and ran his trembling hand across her name following each letter with his fingers.

'I'm sorry... I'm so sorry....'

He rose to his feet and shuffled away.

A broken man.

80C8

๑๙๙ Chapter twenty four ๑๙๙

The tiny Princetown church was full to capacity and the bright sun blazed through the stained windows onto the congregation and the spring flowers that filled every corner.

Sir Thomas Tyrwhitt sat in the front pew with Captain Shortland and Mara, Captain and Judith Sleep, Isaac Hartman, and Rachel holding baby Emily.

Squire Irwin, Thomas, Priscilla and Dorien sat behind them with some of their estate workers while the remaining pews were filled with local and moorland people.

Henrietta and Alex stood and sobbed beside their father at the back of the church and the congregation waited in anticipation and whispered anxiously to each other.

The organist played and four coffins containing the bodies of Sergeant Greaves, two guards and a militiaman were carried reverently into the church by sixteen immaculately dressed Marines who placed them in front of the altar.

The solemn faced clergyman, who two days earlier had christened Emily in such contrasting circumstances, looked up and spoke. 'Without doubt this has been the moor's darkest day and I pray that catastrophes of this magnitude will never happen again,' he said as he bowed his head respectfully. 'There will be a day of reckoning for someone.'

The congregation nodded and murmured their agreement.

Captain Shortland sobbed unashamedly and Mara squeezed his hand.

The clergyman continued. 'Please turn to hymn number 249.'

The congregation rose to their feet and began to sing. *'There is a green hill far away without a city wall, where our dear Lord was crucified he died to save us all.'*

Every member of the congregation had been affected in one way or another by the preceding events and their anguished and yet powerful voices reached beyond the church and out across the moor.

They were heard by Joshua Amos, Giselle and Phinias, the American clergyman, and a small group of prisoners-of-war. Earlier, they had dug the shallow mass grave in an isolated strip of moorland behind the prison to bury their massacred fellow prisoners. The dead prisoners, with only their shirts as shrouds, were nailed down in the roughest of coffins before being buried together.

Joshua wore the new clothes that Giselle had so carefully chosen and bought for him in Tavistock and stood trying to imagine the horrors that had taken place inside the prison and his providence at not being part of it.

The organist continued to play while the four coffins were carried out to the church cemetery and slowly lowered into their graves.

The congregation dispersed in silence and walked past the church towards the road.

The stern faced Chief Revenue Officer sat on his horse while several other Revenue men stood and waited respectfully in front of the open metal gates and imposing granite pillars.

The wind picked up and thick dark clouds raced spectacularly across the sky enveloping Princetown and the surrounding moorland.

As the numbed congregation spilled out onto the road, the Revenue men made their way unnoticed towards their intended victims.

Sitting upright on his horse the Chief Revenue Officer slowly raised his head and spoke out. 'Squire Robert Irwin... Harold Thomson... you are under arrest for smuggling contraband and failing to pay His Majesty's taxes,' he boomed.

While the Chief Revenue Officer edged nearer to them the other Revenue men rushed forward and forcefully grabbed the Squire and Harold Thomson.

'There must be some mistake,' pleaded Squire Irwin as he struggled with his captors. He broke loose and raced towards Captain Sleep.

The Squire grabbed the unsuspecting Captain from behind, placing his hand firmly around his throat. He pulled a single shot pistol from his jacket and held it to the Captain's head.

The congregation stood and gasped in shock and

horror.

'Come on man... what do you expect to achieve with this charade?' asked the Captain firmly.

Harold Thomson, unmoved, looked on in silence.

'I've done nothing... you can't do this to me... I'm innocent,' pleaded the Squire.

Henrietta and Alex ran screaming towards the Revenue men and tore wildly at their jackets as they marched their father away.

'Tell them... Sir Thomas... tell them!' shouted the Squire.

Sir Thomas Tyrwhitt cast a passing glance in the direction of the Chief Revenue Officer and acknowledged him before shaking his head as he climbed into his carriage and pulled away to make the short journey to Tor Royal.

The Squire now turned his attention to his son. 'Thomas, this is all your doing!' he raged.

A woman in the crowd shouted out. 'Filthy cheatin' smugglers.'

'Hang 'em!' shouted another.

'Yeah... hang 'em all!' shouted several more.

Squire Irwin shook his head wildly, released Captain

Sleep, turned the pistol on himself and fired.

He fell to the floor, dead.

The rooks that had gathered on the church roof squawked noisily and flew into the nearby skeletal trees.

Spring came late to the moor.

A stern faced Captain Sleep shook his head as he stepped over the body and walked slowly towards Dorien and Priscilla's carriage.

'I'm sorry about your father... and Mister Cole,' he said caringly to Priscilla.

'Thank you, Captain. Don't blame yourself, you brought him to me,' she said before turning to glare at Captain Shortland and pointing. '*He* took him away,' she said angrily.

'What am I going to do now?' cried Thomas Irwin as he stood and looked at everyone in turn until his eyes fell on to his dead father's body laying in the mud.

'Ah... what have I done!' he cried, his tortured scream reverberating off of the church walls and across the moor.

As the last of the congregation dispersed and the carriages pulled away, the heavens opened and torrential rain hammered onto the lone windswept figure of

Thomas Irwin, his eyes staring out into the unknown and a very uncertain future. Captain Shortland and Mara walked towards the prison oblivious to the storm raging around them.

Her father turned to her. 'Mara... I'm going back to sea,' he sobbed, the rain hiding his tears.

She stopped walking. 'What? After all this time? Are you sure? Are you really sure?' she asked.

Her father nodded and wiped his eyes. 'Yeah... I am... how will I ever forget such wanton carnage? I tried....' He shook his head wildly. 'I had a job to do.' He screwed up his face in disgust and clenched his fists. 'Do you know what they call me?' he placed his finger over her lips before she could answer him. 'Bloody Shortland!' he mouthed. He paused and nodded knowingly, 'perhaps with good reason,' he said. 'Even that bastard, Beasly, did nothing to help... this place is hell itself and I was in charge of it. I'm not a jailer for God's sake, I'm a captain in His Majesty's Navy,' he said forcing an exaggerated smile. 'And I brought you up here,' he said shaking his head and looking around. 'In this Godforsaken place... without a woman around to help me,' he sobbed.

Mara tried desperately to reassure him. 'You did your best, father,' she said softly.

'Did I? Do you really believe that? Ask the dead Yankees and the British guards... the militia and their families... Sergeant Greaves's family... you ask them!' he said, looking around at the mud and the low and heavy clouds sweeping across the prison. 'This place is evil... it changes people... God only knows how many innocent people have died and, after all these years. I still don't know you, my own daughter. You're a woman now, you don't need me... you never have...,' he said, stopping to wipe his eyes.

Mara put her arm around him as they walked back through the prison gates.

Following the massacre, Sir Thomas Tyrwhitt took control of the depot. He suspended the Somerset militia, maintaining control with a handful of Marines and trusted guards, and surprisingly there was little trouble.

With the agreement and help of the Transport Office in Plymouth arrangements were made to repatriate the American prisoners-of-war and it was established that they should leave in groups, decided by drawing lots.

At the end of April 1815, the first draft of 249 ragged

and emaciated but jubilant Americans loaded their meagre belongings onto carts and packed them around the sick and injured.

Dylan Chipp swapped places with Joshua Amos and left along with Big Dick. 'I shan't be sorry to see the back of this vile place,' said Dylan loudly. 'Even if I am broke,' he chuckled, as he walked beneath the carved arch for the last time.

'I's reckon us cun do sum good business, Mister Chipp,' said Big Dick.

'I reckon we can... I reckon we can,' replied Dylan, straightening his threadbare, blood stained jacket.

The cart carried a large flag, which represented the Goddess of Liberty crying over the tomb of the Americans who died, and bore the inscription, "Columbia weeps and will remember."

They all talked excitedly as they marched across the moor and down towards Plymouth and the waiting cartel ships that would take them back to America.

Others barely able to walk struggled to keep up at the rear.

Peter Beck was finally well enough to leave and stood amongst the last batch of prisoners to depart the soon to be deserted depot.

Captain Shortland, holding a bottle of whiskey and supported by the loyal Doctor MacGrath, swayed uncontrollably outside of his office and watched intently.

Mara walked past her father, gently touching his shoulder as she made her way across the yard to join Peter who stood and held tightly onto the cart. He was blindly overawed by the intense activity around him as he was pushed and jostled by his fellow countrymen who eagerly made their final preparations to leave.

'Hello Peter,' said Mara, letting out a deep sigh. 'You're going back with them today?' she asked.

He mumbled as he reached out for her hand but she couldn't hear him.

Much to his surprise she pulled away.

He tilted his head questioningly to one side and she guided his hand towards hers and placed a pair of glasses in it.

'Sorry they took so long. Beasly wouldn't get them for me... so I had them sent from Bath,' she said. 'Are they all right?' she asked anxiously.

Peter smiled as he pulled them around his ears and adjusted them on his nose.

Mara stepped back apprehensively and awaited his reaction.

Gradually the blurred image became clearer and at last he could see her. He smiled and reached out for her hand.

'They're perfect,' he said. 'Perfect.'

He looked at her intensely and she pulled back nervously.

'No... please don't worry,' he said with a smile. 'It's just... you're even more beautiful than I ever remembered...' he paused while he looked at her. 'Much more,' he said softly.

Mara blushed. 'Do you really mean that, Peter?' she asked.

'Yes, Mara... I do,' he whispered softly. 'There's no question.'

'You didn't answer mine,' asked Mara. 'Are you?' she waited for an answer. 'Are you... going back with them?'

Peter hesitated. 'Um... I'm sorry,' he said thoughtfully. 'Going back...? Of course I am.'

She was taken aback by his reply and her eyes filled with tears.

'My mother and father will need me even more now

that Benjamin's gone,' he reflected sadly. Peter choked back his grief and continued. 'But... I'd like you to come with me,' he said, smiling lovingly at her.

'With you...? To America? Are you sure?' she shrieked. 'What about my father?' she said looking across apprehensively at Captain Shortland.

Her father screwed up his face and slowly nodded his agreement to the silent question he knew was being asked before taking another long slug from the bottle and chewing wildly on his cigar.

Mara and Peter reached out for each other and kissed.

'I've lost her, George,' mumbled Captain Shortland.

'She's in very capable hands, Captain,' said the Doctor.

'Um... I know, and I lost this place too,' he said shaking his head. 'I've lost everything.'

'Come, Thomas. Let's have that drink,' coaxed the Doctor as he helped the weeping Captain inside.

The Americans finally left the depot in warm sunshine and taking up the rear were Peter and Mara riding Captain Shortland's horse.

Peter pulled the horse to a halt.

'Mara, I can't leave without saying goodbye to

Benjamin,' he said, unable to hide his sadness. 'Will you show me where they buried him?' he asked.

'Yes, of course I will...,' she said tightening her grip on his waist. 'I thought you would never ask me,' she said softly.

They rode around the perimeter wall and when they reached the burial ground Peter sat in silence and gazed in horror at the vast area before him.

'I heard tell they buried the prisoners in mass graves but...,' he shook his head. 'I thought at least they would have treated those they massacred... with... with some dignity... some respect!'

He screamed, his grief mixed with outrage and anger. 'What do they know of respect?'

They dismounted and Peter looked out across the expanse of recently dug ground and as the tears streamed down his face he shook his head violently.

'I'm sorry, Peter...!' she screamed.

Mara made to put her arms around him but he pushed her aside.

'I'm... so very sorry!' she cried.

Peter moved closer to the unmarked grave.

He knelt and, overshadowed by the huge granite wall

behind him, said a prayer for his young brother. He reached forward, grabbed a handful of soil, placed it in his handkerchief, folded it and slid it into his jacket pocket.

He sobbed uncontrollably as Mara took his arm. 'Come, Peter, Benjamin's at peace now,' she said softly. 'He's at peace.'

She led him to the horse, they remounted and rode off in silence.

They rejoined the rest of the Americans and made their way slowly through Princetown.

As the last of the American prisoners entered the village square, the subdued townspeople, children and guards that had gathered to watch them leave, stood in silence. They knew they now all faced a very uncertain future.

Mara turned to look for her father but he was nowhere to be seen. In her heart she knew she would never see him again and as she fought back her tears her arms tightened around Peter's waist.

Giselle and Phinias watched from high on the Tor as the last group passed beneath them and crossed the open moor.

Joshua stopped to wave and nodded his appreciation to them before turning to join his fellow Americans.

This was the final group of American prisoners-of war to embark on the last cartel ship and set off for home in June 1815, six months to the day after the peace Treaty of Ghent was signed.

Giselle and Phinias sat in silence staring deep into the fire.

There was a knock at the cottage door and Phinias got up and opened it.

He looked at the caller and smiled the widest grin. 'Cum in,' he said. 'Giselle, us 'ave a visitor,' he shouted.

Phinias and the visitor entered the dimly lit room.

'I changed ma mind,' said Joshua nervously. 'I couldn't leave ya,' he murmured, as he walked towards Giselle.

Giselle stood and looked directly into his eyes. 'I knows,' she said confidently before breaking into a wide smile.

While they hugged each other Giselle held the effigy of Joshua behind his back and squeezed it gently.

'I knawed I was right. 'Ee belongs 'ere with us,' she said softly, ''ee really do.'

Graham Sclater

ഇൻ **The end** ഇൻ

෨෫ Epilogue ෨෫

In March 1815, on the other side of the English Channel, Napoleon left Elba and France was once again at war with England. This time the hostilities were short lived as he was defeated at Waterloo and many of the French were captured. Bizarrely some of those captured at Ligny had been released from the Dartmoor depot, less than two years earlier, and were once again to be incarcerated in the prison.

On April 6, 1815, several months after the war had ended; many American prisoners were massacred or wounded by the British within the Dartmoor depot and shortly after an Anglo-American commission awarded compensation to the families of those who died there.

Soon after the release of the French prisoners-of-war in June 1816 the Dartmoor depot was closed for more than twenty years, to be reopened in 1850 as a civilian prison for dangerous convicts sentenced to life and hard labour and earning a worldwide reputation of being one of the most infamous convict prisons.

Dartmoor Prison is still in use today and memorials have been erected for all the American and French prisoners-of-war who died there.

ജ്യൈ

Tabitha Books

*Due for publication in 2010
by Tabitha Books*

Receivers

By

Graham Sclater

Tabitha Books

Preface

It is spring 2010 and over the past twelve months companies that had previously been extremely profitable succumbed to the recession that was spreading rampantly throughout the British Isles like some kind of uncontrollable disease or virus.

No area of business was safe.

Despite the deepening recession, Brian and Sylvia Chapman battled against the odds to keep their dream alive, to stay in business. Following major cash flow problems, the company's bankers decided to withdraw their financial support as they had done with so many companies during this period.

The liquidation of the company and the ensuing problems faced by them and their family, from employees, creditors, the Receivers, and the banks - in fact, from everyone - leads to a devastating and harrowing period resulting in disastrous consequences.

£

Chapter one

Who will buy?

The vast tarmac car park that had been completely deserted earlier was now filling rapidly and a line of queuing cars choked the nearby roads causing near chaos for other road users.

In the heavy rain and strong winds, the impatient drivers eventually began to pull in, and fought to fill the spaces nearest to the main building. The occupants rushed out of their cars and joined the ever-growing crowd pushing their way towards the double doors.

As the rusty and faded light green 1984-registered Ford Escort turned into the car park, the driver braked hard and blocked the entrance. He pushed himself hard back into the seat and in sheer disbelief, shook his head violently, as he tried to take in the chaotic scenes around him. At the same time he tried desperately to keep the engine ticking over dropped the clutch and teased the accelerator pedal. Unable to hold back his feelings any longer he screamed angrily, the deafening roar reverberating around the car.

'Bloody leeches, they didn't waste any sodding time!' he raged.

His lapse in concentration caused the car to shudder to a standstill and it took several attempts before the engine turned over and he was finally able to make his way into the car park.

He drove around frantically until he found the only remaining free space at the far side of the car park near to the group of vans that were now surrounded by people. As he manoeuvred into the space he scratched a shiny black BMW parked to his left. His car stalled and he sat looking out through the dirty and cracked windscreen. He tried desperately to calm down, oblivious to the damage he had inflicted on the adjacent vehicle.

Finding it extremely difficult to breathe he fumbled in the pockets of his jacket until he found his Ventolin inhaler. Pulling it from his pocket, he pushed it between his narrow lips and squeezed it several times before the effects of the drug took effect. He moved awkwardly across to the passenger seat and pushed open the door. Realising that he did not have enough room to squeeze out of the car he reluctantly climbed back over the gear stick and hand brake into the driver's seat. He searched the glove compartment until he found the broken window winder and held it in place with his left hand while he wound down the window and then reached for the outside door handle. The rusty and dented door creaked loudly as he tried in vain to push it open. Getting more frustrated he slid down into the seat pushed his shoulder against the door until it swung forcefully into the van parked alongside it, the impact denting the bodywork.

Relieved, he now stood in the car park beside his car looking strangely out of place compared to the other drivers who were now making their way excitedly towards the building.

He was a short man, in his early forties, with unbrushed collar length greasy hair, deep furrowed lines in his forehead, unshaven with bloodshot eyes and wearing an expensive creased and ripped suede jacket. His hand-made, Italian mud splattered black shoes and badly creased dark green ill-fitting trousers appeared an unusual combination.

As he walked between the dirty commercial vehicles he subconsciously ran his finger down the side of the nearest van to reveal unblemished navy blue paintwork. Noticing the result of his effort he took a dirty handkerchief from his jacket pocket and worked energetically rubbing the dirt to reveal the clean silver signwriting along the side of the van. Overcome with emotion he choked back the tears, kicked at the tyres and walked blindly towards the front entrance. With his back bent and his narrow shoulders drooping forward, he picked his way between the last row of cars, stopping only for a brief moment to look up at the crookedly nailed, hand painted sign - *Auction today.* Above it was a very impressive, large, bright, rectangular sign fixed to the side of the building - *Brian Chapman Maintenance Services.*

Bending his head even lower he stooped unnecessarily, and walked through the entrance.

The large crowd that had already assembled inside the building were packed tightly together in what was previously the main office. Desks, chairs, filing cabinets, computers and all manner of office equipment were marked with a Lot number and spread all around the office. The bespectacled middle aged auctioneer stood, on a makeshift platform, a foot or so above them and checked to see that anyone interested in the auction was inside. After clearing his throat, he began. 'Lot one - a four drawer filing cabinet. Let's start the bidding at twenty pounds.'

In the front of the crowd, a young man shyly waved his catalogue while the auctioneer looked around the room for other interest. Although an overweight man joined in the bidding, at sixty-five pounds, he lost interest, allowing the younger man to complete the purchase and to smile nervously at the people nearest to him.

During the bidding for the first item, the dishevelled man pushed his way around the perimeter of the crowd. Finding a place in a dark corner, he removed a small notebook and pen from his inside pocket and began to write down the price of every item as it was sold.

The man in the shadows cursed under his breath as the auctioneer looked around the room and repeated the figure again. 'Thirty pounds, do I hear thirty five?'

A young man raised his hand but the young woman, after hesitating for a split second, continued to bid.

On the podium, the auctioneer sensed that the battle was almost over. 'Ninety five pounds, am I bid one hundred?' He looked around the room but the interest had now diminished. 'Going once, going twice.' He raised his hand and smashed the gavel onto the desk. 'The last Lot of the day... sold for ninety five pounds.'

The lady smiled and walked towards the auctioneer's clerk.

'Ladies and gentlemen that concludes today's auction. I would like to thank you on behalf of the Receivers and would remind you that any items purchased today, must be paid for and removed within the next hour. There will be a number of auctions of a similar nature in the next few days and I would suggest that you review the local press, our web site, or telephone our office.' He forced a tired smile and closed his book. 'Thank you.'

While the dishevelled man remained in the corner and concentrated on totalling the figures the remaining members of the public shuffled over towards the clerk to pay for the items that they had bought.

The man shook his head and mumbled to himself. 'Six thousand, five hundred and twenty four pounds and fifty sodding pence, that's not going to go very bloody far.'

He pushed the notebook and pen into his pocket and walked through the remaining empty and deserted offices. Looking into the last office he noticed a photograph on the floor behind the glazed door and bent down to pick it up but as he stopped to look at it the auctioneer's assistant walked into the room and confronted him. 'Can I help you, mate? What are you doing in here?'

Still holding the photograph the man tried to hide it behind his back. 'It's alright, it belongs to me,' he mumbled.

'I think you must be mistaken, sir?' questioned the auctioneer's assistant.

'No... it is mine. I'm just having one last look ar... ' mumbled the man in response to his interrogator.

The auctioneer's assistant interrupted him. 'Oh yeah... you are... are you?' he humoured him and smiled falsely.

The man replied in an almost inaudible voice, 'I'm....' He cleared his throat and continued, 'I'm...I'm Brian Chapman.'

The auctioneer's assistant was taken aback and continued to stare, and not totally sure that the stranger was telling the truth, continued to interrogate him. 'So you're... Brian Chapman eh?'

The stranger nodded, gave a forced smile, handed him the photograph and pointed at a smartly dressed man in the centre. The auctioneer's assistant cast his eye over the scruffy man standing in front of him. He studied the photograph more closely for a few seconds and finally satisfied with the man's explanation handed it back.

'OK... nice offices, it's a pity we didn't get more for this stuff and your vans. Mind you,' he paused, '...yours is the ninth this week, you can't give anything away these days.'

Brian stared at him while he felt in his pocket for his notebook. 'I know,' he mouthed.

He gave a half smile, turned, and walked out of the room and down the corridor that had been his pride and joy for the last thirteen years. He stopped walking and glanced briefly at the photograph that had been taken only a few months earlier at the annual company dinner. He mumbled to himself. 'Those were the days.'

He took one last look around the office and as he felt the tears welling up, walked slowly towards the main doors.

The auctioneer's assistant called after him. 'Bye, Mr Chapman.'

Without any acknowledgement or response Brian walked out of the building.

Now standing alone, he pulled the filthy handkerchief from his pocket and wiped his eyes.

He took a deep breath, straightened his back and walked slowly across the now deserted car park towards his Escort.

The grey sky darkened and the rain laden clouds driven on by the strong south westerly wind built up above him and it started to rain heavily. Still clutching the rolled up photograph, he made a pathetic attempt to protect himself from the elements by pulling his narrow jacket collar up around his neck, and ran towards his car.

An ear-splitting shot reverberated across the car park and the photograph, propelled by the gust of wind, blew out of Brian's hand as he fell to the ground.

£

To be continued